I'm sitting in the shed with a bottle of Coke and a packet of crisps. It's been a week and I've almost given up hope of ever getting a client. Seven days ago it seemed like the best idea I'd ever had. A private eye for teenagers. I figured that if adults had all these problems then teenagers must have them too. And being adolescents these problems would probably be in spades. They just didn't have the money to pay as much. But, hey, I was just starting out. I could afford to be cheap.

Who was I kidding? I didn't have any other choice.

'Dominic Barker's debut novel is wittily written in a style that spoofs Raymond Chandler . . . Barker knows what he is doing and deserves to be a hit' *Sunday Times*

'A smart debut, packed with funny lines' *Observer*

'A clever and witty story which has many modern themes to engage contemporary readers' *School Librarian*

'Lively and funny with an all-too-sharp picture of school life' *Children's Book News, Book Trust*

Also available by Dominic Barker

SHARP SHOT

To Carol

SHARP STUFF
A CORGI BOOK: 0 552 547840

First publication in Great Britain

PRINTING HISTORY
Corgi edition published 1999
Reissued 2001

Set in 12/15.5pt Palatino by
Phoenix Typesetting, Ilkley, West Yorkshire.

Corgi Yearling Books are published by Transworld Publishers,
61–63 Uxbridge Road, London W5 5SA,
a division of The Random House Group Ltd,
in Australia by Random House Australia (Pty) Ltd,
20 Alfred Street, Milsons Point, NSW 2061, Australia,
in New Zealand by Random House New Zealand Ltd,
18 Poland Road, Glenfield, Auckland 10, New Zealand,
and in South Africa by Random House (Pty) Ltd,
Endulini, 5a Jubilee Road, Parktown 2193, South Africa.

Printed and bound in Great Britain by
Cox & Wyman Ltd, Reading, Berkshire.

SHARP STUFF

A MICKEY SHARP CASE

DOMINIC BARKER

CORGI BOOKS

CHAPTER ONE

I'm sitting in the shed with a bottle of Coke and a packet of crisps. It's been a week and I've almost given up hope of ever getting a client. Seven days ago it seemed like the best idea I'd ever had. A private eye for teenagers. I figured that if adults had all these problems then teenagers must have them too. And being adolescents these problems would probably be in spades. They just didn't have the money to pay as much. But, hey, I was just starting out. I could afford to be cheap.

Who was I kidding? I didn't have any other choice.

It's beginning to look like being cheap isn't going to be enough. Nobody has come and nobody looks like coming. Maybe my advert was wrong. I put it in all the shop windows in town and all the free papers.

PRIVATE EYE SEEKS CASES...

ANYTHING CONSIDERED IN LOCAL AREA - CONFIDENTIALITY GUARANTEED - I'M 14 SO I'M VERY CHEAP.

CONTACT:
MICKEY SHARP
THE SHED
THE BACK GARDEN
32 WAKE GREEN ROAD
HANFORD

It's the address that bothers me the most. Would you take a personal problem to a boy in a shed? I'm not sure I would.

I take a critical glance around it. It's kind of my place these days. My room's OK but there's not too much privacy. Someone's always barging in on you. Because I'm the youngest, nobody in my family seems to think I've got any rights. Walk into my sister's room without knocking one day and see what happens to you. It won't be pretty. So, I hang around here a lot when I'm at home.

Umair, my best mate, used to come round until his parents stopped him. I've got a cassette player and a dart board and a couple of old chairs down here in the shed. I even dusted it out – first time I'd ever really cleaned anything properly. It's harder than it looks. Since I decided to become a detective I've even got an old desk in here. It had been lying round the garage for years but I thought that you need a desk if you want to look like you mean business. And you can put your feet up on it when you're thinking. But whatever I've done with the place it is still a shed. And the thing about sheds is that they just don't look professional.

I'm kicking these thoughts around in my head and thinking glumly that I'll have to go back to train-spotting when she walks in.

She's at least fifteen and she moves like she knows it. She's tall but not as tall as me. She's wearing jeans, Nikes and a cut-off top that shows her stomach. She's got long hair, dark brown eyes and no visible acne. I'd be prepared to listen to her all day.

'Are you Mickey Sharp?' she says. Her

voice is smooth and dark, like posh chocolate. 'Am I in the right place?'

I assure her she is. I hope I'm not looking surprised. She sits down on a box and crosses her legs.

'My name's Madeleine Stone. I've come to you about my brother,' she says huskily.

'Hold on,' I say.

I'm so surprised at getting a client that I almost forget to take notes. It's one of the things detectives do. I've seen it on the TV. I open the drawer of my desk and pull out my notebook and a pen. I flick the book open.

'Tell me the whole story,' I say. 'Take your time and try not to leave anything out.'

She looks impressed. I'm pleased because that's the whole idea.

'My brother,' she says, and then she stops. She's looking round the shed. I can see doubt beginning to cross her mind.

'You do know what you're doing, don't you?' she says.

'Sure,' I say, trying to sound much more confident than I feel.

'How would a girl know?' she asks, fixing

her dark brown eyes onto mine. I try not to gulp.

'You'll know when I solve your case. But I can't solve it until you tell me about it.' I stare at her. She stares back. 'What have you got to lose?' I ask.

That shot goes home. She shrugs.

'Your brother?' I remind her.

'I think he's being horribly bullied.'

I try not to look relieved. I've got her to tell me about the case. 'Why?' I ask.

'He's changed. He used to be happy and friendly and now he just sits about the house and doesn't talk to anyone. He hardly ever comes out of his room and he looks so sad all the time. It's terrible.'

'Maybe he's just going through a phase,' I say. This is my father's standard explanation for the behaviour of anyone under eighteen.

This line doesn't go down too well with Madeleine. Her face hardens up all of a sudden.

'Don't be pathetic,' she snaps.

She starts to stand up. I panic. I can't lose her now.

'When did it start?' I ask quickly.

11

She looks down at me. She doesn't go and she doesn't exactly stay.

'The bullying,' I remind her.

She stares at me for what seems a very long time and then sits down again. I breathe a sigh of relief. I'm not going to lose my first client after all.

'About six weeks after he started at St John's,' she says. 'I know something bad is happening to him there. If you saw him now you wouldn't believe what fun he used to be. He was so clever and. . .'

'OK, OK.' I cut her short this time. I've already heard enough about her little brother's lost charms. He sounds like those kids who sit up at the front of the class and always know the answers.

'Are there any other signs he's being bullied?' I ask.

'Oh yes. He's got some terribly big bruises on his arms.' She leans forward and touches my arm as she says it.

'Has he told you he's been bullied?'

She shakes her head. 'He won't talk to anyone anymore but I just know that he is.'

'Why don't you tell your parents about it?'

'You don't know my brother. If I told my parents, he'd go crazy and then he'd deny it all. He's very stubborn. And my parents are always so busy anyway.'

'But if he was being bullied. . . Surely they'd do something?' I say.

'Is that your business?' she snaps at me. 'I thought you just did what the client told you.'

'OK. Whatever you say.' I pull back and put my hands in the air. She is one touchy girl and I don't want her running away.

There's a silence. After a while I break it or we'd both have got old and died in that shed.

'Well, what would you like me to do about it?'

'I'd like you to stop it. I want my old little brother back again.'

'Well, I'll do my best.'

She seems to lighten up once I've agreed to look into it. She tells me his name, where they live and from her purse she pulls out a picture of him and hands it to me. I look at it. She's on the picture too. I take her number.

She stands up to go. We still haven't discussed money. I take a deep breath.

'I charge five pounds a day plus expenses.'

She stares at me. Her face suddenly looks much harder.

'Three pounds a day,' I say weakly.

'Mickey,' she says. 'I can't afford the price you're asking right now but let me tell you. . .'

'Two pounds,' I offer.

She keeps on talking. 'Let me assure you that if I get my little brother back like he was I would be grateful to whoever saved him.'

Her eyes are very wide and she's looking at me like I'm the most important person on earth.

'Very grateful.'

I know I should say no. I know I should insist on her agreeing to pay. I know I should try to maintain some kind of professional relationship. But when you're fourteen years old and there's a beautiful girl in your shed, you sometimes say yes when you shouldn't.

When she's gone, I lean back on my chair and put my feet on the desk. There's no better position to think. Teachers don't understand that though. Lean back on your chair and straight away they're yelling at you about how much the chair costs the school and how much you're going to damage it. Put your feet on the desk and they get even worse. 'Do you put your feet on the furniture at home, Sharp?' That's a dumb question if you ask me. Everybody puts their feet on the furniture at home. They may not do it when their mother's in the room but they all do it. Even teachers do it. Not that they admit it though.

I stare at the picture. I'm supposed to be remembering what the kid looks like but I spend more of my time looking at the half of the picture which contains Madeleine. She's walked out of the shed leaving some big questions in my mind. Why is she so concerned about her little brother? Has she told me the truth about why she won't tell her parents about what she thinks is happening to him? And how does she feel about relationships with younger boys?

I snap out of my daydream. Thinking about Madeleine isn't going to get me anywhere. I look at the other half of the picture, the bit with the kid in. He looks like a normal kid. Sometimes it's funny-looking kids who attract bullies, kids with glasses or spots or something but there's nothing in Madeleine's brother's face to make you think he's going to get hassled.

Bullying's a weird thing. You beat up some kid who's littler than you and who's got no chance of getting back at you. Why? What does it prove? I can't find an answer to that one.

Still, trying to work out why some people want to bully other people isn't my problem. I have to find out whether it's happening to this kid, who's doing it and then try to stop them. I figure that the first two shouldn't be too difficult. All I have to do is follow the kid and see what happens to him. Bullies aren't known for their subtlety and if the kid is getting bruises all over him somebody has to be giving them to him and all I have to do is be there when it's happening.

Stopping the bullying is a different thing. That could be tricky. The only reliable way of stopping a bully is to grow a lot or move house. Then you're bigger than him or living in a different city and he's got to leave you alone. I get the feeling that neither of these is the start of a good plan.

I saw an American talk show once. There was this psychologist on it. He was saying that we should feel sorry for bullies because they didn't get enough love and stuff when they were little and so they've grown up all mean and hard. They treat other people badly because that's what they were taught. The way to stop a bully, this guy reckoned, is to show him that you care about him. When enough people have shown the bully that they care about him then he'll stop bullying. Everybody in the audience whooped and jumped up and down when he said that and the psychologist guy smiled like he was the cleverest person in the world. The thing is, I'd like to see him tell some of the psychos in my school that he cared about them. They'd put him in hospital.

All this thinking isn't getting me any nearer the answer to the big question of how you stop people bullying one another. I check my watch. It's almost six thirty. I wander into my house. Maybe someone in my family could help me. There's got to be a first time for everything.

I keep trying to bring the subject up during dinner. The trouble is that it's hard to get a word in edgeways. Karen, my sister, and my dad disagree about everything and the dinner table is the place where they do it. They hardly talk to each other the rest of the time but my mum insists that we all eat together. 'The family that eats together, stays together,' she told me once. 'The family that eats together, screams together' is more like what happens in our house.

Today it's their favourite subject, modelling. Dad puts his knife and fork down which means we are in for a big performance.

'What does the average person think of a model? I'll tell you what the average person thinks of a model. They think they're brainless bodies. Why? Because they never say anything and they just have clothes hung on them. Walking clothes-pegs. Is that what you want to be?'

My sister wants to be a model. She keeps nagging them to give her the money to get a portfolio of photos done and she's stopped eating her dinner. I don't know why she bothers. They haven't got any money and she's got lousy posture. She sags when she walks.

'How do you know they're brainless? That's just prejudice.'

'Prejudice' is one of my sister's favourite words. She's doing GCSE Sociology.

'No, it isn't. When did you ever see one of them say something intelligent? Never. They talk about make-up and clothes and that's it.'

'You've never met one. You wouldn't know.'

'And how much do they get paid? Fortunes. When there's much more important things happening in the world.'

My dad doesn't like people earning lots of money.

'They do things for charity,' says my sister.

'Showing off and feeling good about it. That's what they do. They don't care about anything but what they see in the mirror.'

'You don't know that.'

'Let's all calm down,' says my mum.

She may as well have been talking to the wall.

'Don't tell me what I do or don't know, young lady,' snaps my dad, completely ignoring my mum.

Things are now going to get ugly. My

sister objects very strongly to being called a lady.

'I've told you not to call me that.'

I wish she hadn't said 'told'.

'Nobody tells me what to do in my own house. Is "lady" a swear word? No, it is not. It's a perfectly reasonable word.'

'You don't understand.'

'Oh, I don't do I? Of course I wouldn't. I'm probably out of touch. Not "with it". Left behind. Unable to understand.'

My dad gets like this a lot these days. He lost his job about two years ago and he hasn't had another one since. He's only 47 but he talks like he's 100. It can get very boring at times.

There's a silence at the table. They've blown themselves out. I decide to get my question in fast.

'How do you stop a bully bullying someone?'

Nobody answers. I figure they're thinking of what to say but then my father gets up and says he's going to watch the news. Then my mother and sister start talking about my sister's ex-boyfriend. I give up and go up to my room.

That's my family for you. About as much use as a French textbook in a Maths lesson.

CHAPTER TWO

The next morning I'm up early. If I'm going to follow this kid I'm going to have to tail him from outside his house, otherwise I'll never find him. I get my bike and ride down to Madeleine's house by seven forty-five. I watch the house. Their house is bigger than ours. The garden's a mess and there are two cars outside. That's about it. Houses are boring things to watch and ten minutes go by like they've got lead weights on. Even Geography goes faster than this. There's a big highlight after fifteen minutes when the milkman comes. They have three pints. Then the father comes out and gets in one car and drives off. Then the mother. It's eight twenty by now and I am really fed up. I knew it wasn't going to be all glamour but I could do with a little excitement right now.

There's no sign of Madeleine. I don't know which school she goes to. She can't go to the same school as her brother because St John's is all boys. I wouldn't fancy going to an all-boys school. Schools are boring enough places and you need all the variety you can get. I try to work out which is her bedroom but I can't tell.

I figure that they must be richer than us. Apart from their house being bigger, they've got two cars. We've only got one and that's falling to bits. Since my dad lost his job we haven't really been able to get too many new things. I don't mention it though because my mum says it makes my dad depressed. If he's not normally depressed, I'd really hate to see him when he is, so I try to keep my mouth shut. It's hard sometimes though, I just talk about wanting things without thinking and then I feel lousy about it. Sometimes I think it might be better not to say anything at all.

Finally, the kid comes out. Brown hair, normal height – he's exactly like his photo except he's got his school uniform on. Macauley Stone. Parents shouldn't be allowed to give kids names like Macauley. It's just asking for trouble. I reckon some names should have health warnings like cigarettes do. 'Call your child this and he will be cussed non-stop at school from the age of five to sixteen and probably screwed up for life.'

Parents never learn though. My uncle and aunt had a baby last year and they called him Sebastian. I ask you, Sebastian. We went to the christening. The baby howled right through it, he probably heard what they were calling him.

Afterwards, we went back to the house and everyone was cooing over him and passing him round. They made me hold him. I didn't want to but they made me. And I looked at him and felt sorry for him. He didn't know all the trouble that was waiting for him in the future because of that name. Maybe he'll be lucky. Maybe he'll start using his middle name before it's too late. But I doubt it.

Anyway, I follow Macauley which isn't too hard. There are kids in school uniform all over the place at this time so I don't stand out. The one thing about him that you don't get from his photo is his walk. He's like one of those electric toys you get for Christmas when you're about six, the ones that break in about three days. You put some batteries in, press the 'on' button and off they go. And their walk is kind of dumb and slow but you know that they'll keep going for ever or until they hit a wall. There's something about Macauley's walk which reminds me of those toys. He just keeps plodding on.

So, we go to his school which is about a mile away and in the opposite direction to mine. And all the way I'm half-waiting for someone to stop him but nobody does. I don't really know what to do if something does happen to him. I'm not too crazy about charging in and trying to save him – I'm a detective not a bodyguard – but then I won't feel too good about just standing there and watching him get knocked about. Fortunately, I don't have to make my mind up because nothing happens to him. We get to his school and he goes in and that's it. I'm not really too surprised. If you're a big kid and you're bullying a little kid it's not like you're going to get up especially early to do it – he isn't going anywhere, is he? I turn my bike around and pedal like crazy to get into my school before first period.

*   *   *

I get to school about five minutes before the end of registration. You've got to be careful when you're going in late because sometimes Walton's wandering round. He's the head and one of his favourite hobbies is catching kids who are coming in late. If he catches you he yells at you. He loves yelling. 'Sharp,' he'll yell, 'you make me sick, lad.' And he gets one of his fingers and he pokes you in the chest. He's got really tough fingers and it hurts. You wouldn't believe one finger could hurt so much. I think he does exercises with it. Some kid's dad came up once to complain about it, said that it was assault or something. Walton told him he was emphasizing a point to his child and that he had touched him accidentally, which is funny because he's been having the same accident for years.

It's worse if he's caught you before and he's caught *me* loads of times. After he's yelled at you and poked you a bit he makes you do a job for him. He'll give you a bin liner and make you pick up all the litter off the field. It's a disgusting job. I don't even like to think about some of the things that lie around our school field but you don't see too many sliding tackles when kids are playing football.

I lock my bike up and go in by the door by the science blocks. It's the furthest away from Walton's office. I pass a couple of teachers but they don't say anything. Most of them can't be bothered unless it's a fight or something. You can't blame them. If they had to try to sort out everything that went wrong in our school they'd never get any teaching done.

I go into our classroom and get the usual cheer of 'Detention' from the morons on the back row. Kids are their own worst enemies. Instead of sticking together we spend most of our time getting each other into trouble. We're just playing into the teachers' hands.

I ignore all the shouting and try to keep my face looking sorrowful for Mr Newman. He's our latest form teacher, the second one we've had this year already. We've had five altogether. Some kids say that the others had nervous breakdowns but they're making it up. All we know is that they've just gone one morning and there is another one in their place and nobody will tell you why.

Newman's lasted longer than I expected. He's pretty young for a teacher. He gives me this look when I walk in. I tell him I'm sorry. He says that this is the second time this week and it's not good enough. I tell him my bike had a flat tyre. The class give me a whole load of stick when I say that and start yelling at Newman that I'm lying and he should put me in detention. With friends like this you don't need enemies. Then, Katie Pierce really finishes me off by saying, 'Sir, Mickey said he had a flat tyre on Monday. He's just making it up.'

Katie Pierce has always had it in for me, I've never worked out why. Trouble is, I realize that she's right and this shows I'm not concentrating. Never use the same excuse twice in the same week even if it's true. It's always going to arouse suspicion. Newman gives me this long stare as if to say, 'Explain that one then, Sharp.' I shrug my shoulders.

So he starts off on this lecture about punctuality and how important it is and how it's the same as politeness and how you've got to discipline yourself to be on time because if you don't then you'll never get a job. All the usual stuff. But you can tell he doesn't believe it any more than I do. But I nod every now and then and look serious. It normally works.

This time it doesn't though. He gives me late detention which gets a big cheer from the morons at the back. This is a pain because I want to follow Macauley home and see if anything happened to him. Late detention's dead boring. You go and sit in a room for half an hour with a whole load of other kids who were late and a deputy head. Nobody's allowed to speak, read or even work. I don't know what lesson they think this is teaching us but whatever it is it doesn't work too well because it's the same faces every night.

I try one last protest to Mr Newman but it doesn't do any good so I go and sit down.

'Where you been?' Umair asks me.

'Nowhere,' I tell him.

He looks at me for a second and then goes back to his magazine.

There was a time when I would have told him what was happening but not any more. We used to be good mates but then we stopped. His parents told him to keep away from me so we don't see too much of each other any more. Being Umair, he does what his mum and dad say. We still sit together in registration but that's all.

It's not really his fault. His mum and dad are really on his back about doing well at school. They check his homework every night and they ring up the school about twice a week to make sure he's doing all right. I'd go mad if my mum and dad were like that but Umair hardly ever moans. They want him to be a lawyer. They've decided what university they want him to go to already. You need to get 'A's in everything for your entire life to get in there. I said to his dad once that there must be easier ways to get to wear a wig but he didn't think it was funny.

Anyway, one time when his mum and dad were up at school, some teacher told them that I was a bad influence on him and that I distracted him during lessons so they banned him from talking to me. At first I figured that it would be just during lessons and that we'd still hang out at breaktime and stuff but that's not how it turned out. He joined the chess club. I'll do a lot of things to keep a friendship going but playing chess every lunchtime isn't one of them.

So, now we never talk apart from registration and hardly ever then. I reckon we'd both like to move places but neither of us will because it would be admitting we weren't friends any more. But we won't sit together in registration next year, that's for sure.

The bell goes and everybody heads off. I catch up with Newman in the corridor and try to convince him that he doesn't really want to put me in detention but he just walks off.

By the end of the day I'm weighing up whether to go or not. I had another go at Newman at afternoon registration. I told him that I had to go round to my grandmother's and mow her lawn because she was ill at the moment. He just laughed sarcastically and said that he reckoned he'd be aiding her recovery by not letting me go and see her. Some teachers just don't have a heart.

So, now I have to decide whether it's worth missing. If you don't go to late detention, they double it and if you don't go then, they ring your parents. They used to write but it's too easy to intercept the letters. So now they ring.

The thought of Madeleine makes up my

mind for me. There are loads of detentions in this world but only one Madeleine. I decide that impressing her is priority number one. I bunk my last class, which is French, and it doesn't exactly break my heart and head off down to Macauley's school.

Bunking lessons is easy. The secret is confidence. You walk straight out of the main gate looking like you are doing nothing wrong and it's fine. Most kids when they're bunking out of school start diving behind hedges every time they see a teacher and crawling around on their stomachs like they are in the SAS or something. It's a waste of time and it gets you dirty. And also if a teacher sees you diving behind a hedge he knows you're up to something so he'll come and find out what. Walking straight out past them is much more reliable. Hardly anybody ever stops you but if they do you just say you're going to the dentist and that normally works. If it doesn't, of course, you're completely stuck and you might as well look forward to spending the rest of your life in detention. You could try fainting I suppose but I wouldn't hold out much hope. Mind you, I don't bunk school very often. Teachers notice that you're not there if you do it too much and then one thing leads to another and before you know it you're sitting in Walton's office with your mum and dad and they're all shouting at you at once and telling you you're a waste of space. That's the kind of scene I like to miss. But bunking off every once in a while is normally OK.

Anyway, today it goes according to plan except that when I go past the last classroom before the street, I notice that Newman's teaching in there. But he doesn't see me. At least, I'm pretty sure he doesn't.

Three fifteen and I'm outside Macauley's school waiting to follow him home. I've taken off my tie because the Hanford High uniform isn't the most popular sight down by St John's. They're Catholics, we're not, so we're supposed to hit one another or something. Makes no sense to me. There isn't that much trouble these days but it isn't worth looking for, is it?

So, the kid comes out and off we go again. He's walking home with this friend. And that's all they do. They split up about two roads from home when Macauley's mate goes into his house and that's it. Straight home. No stops. No bullies. Nothing. Maybe he is powered by batteries. Macauley's obviously one single-minded kid. I could have gone to detention after all.

I ride back home and go and sit in my office and drink a can of Coke. And then I drink another. One day on the case and one detention, one bunked class and no leads. Success is not a word which leaps to mind.

CHAPTER THREE

The next morning I'm outside Macauley's house again. I don't think I'm going to get anywhere but I can't think of anything else to do. I've got nothing to lose. I've already got an hour's detention tonight and they can't give you any more because it's against the law or something. I know because Mr Barlow tried to put Katie Pierce in detention for an hour and a half once for vandalizing his Venn diagram during Maths. She stood up in front of the whole class and said that he couldn't and if he tried she'd tell her mother. Katie Pierce's mother is a local councillor and she's a governor of the school. She came in once and gave us a talk about how we shouldn't smoke. She goes mad if any teacher tries to give Katie any grief. Mr Barlow looked really angry but after the lesson he called Katie back and said he'd decided to let her off this time.

I've been waiting about twenty minutes

and I'm losing my concentration. The truth is that I'm thinking about Madeleine again. I can't seem to get her eyes out of my mind. Suddenly I look up and there's a police car pulling up right next to me. I haven't done anything but I suddenly think I have. That's the trouble with the police. As soon as they show an interest in you, you start thinking you're a criminal. There're two cops in there and they give me this long stare. Then one beckons to me with his finger. 'Over here, sonny.'

I walk over wearing my most innocent smile.

'We've had a phone call which tells us that you've been loitering in this area for the past two days. You want to tell us why?'

'Two days,' I say, acting confused. 'I've not been here two days.'

'Don't get funny with me, sonny. I've been up all night and I'm not in the mood.'

'Oh dear,' I say, trying to look sympathetic.

The policeman starts to go red. 'I've been up all night because I've been on duty and I want no more of your lip.'

'Sorry, I was worried about you.'

The policeman goes redder. 'Look, lad, I want to know what you've been doing round here and I want to know now.'

I'm about to tell him when someone starts shouting from behind me.

'That's him, officer, that's the lout who's been leaning on my wall for the past two days.'

I turn round. Coming towards me, waving a walking stick, is an old man in a dressing gown. He must have just left his breakfast because the dressing gown has egg yolk all down the front.

He keeps staring at me but he's shouting at the police officer.

'Thank goodness you got here in time or who knows what he might have done. He was obviously planning a vicious crime.'

The old guy obviously watches too much *Crimewatch*.

'You spilt your breakfast,' I tell him helpfully.

'Be quiet,' he says. 'Children should be seen and not heard.'

I point out that he could see me and he couldn't hear me and he'd still called the police. He starts waving his walking stick at me when I say that.

'Now, now, sir,' says the cop. 'We don't want to hurt anyone, do we?'

'A man must defend his property against intruders,' says the old guy. 'An Englishman's home is his castle.'

I offer the opinion that his home looked more like a bungalow. It doesn't help.

'Officer, arrest this villain and lock him up.'

'Well, I can understand your annoyance, sir, but what has he done?' says the cop. He's beginning to look like he wishes he was somewhere else.

'He has vandalized my wall.'

'Oh,' says the cop. 'Where?'

'I don't know exactly. I thought finding evidence was your job. I, as a public-spirited citizen, merely report the crime.'

'Well, I can't see any vandalism, sir.'

'You haven't even got out of the car. Sherlock Holmes did not solve all his crimes from the front seat of a patrol car, you know, young man.'

'There's no need for that attitude, sir,' says the cop. I am beginning to feel sorry for him.

'No need for that attitude? No need for that attitude? I will have you know, Officer, that I am chairman of the local Neighbourhood Watch. I shall write to the Chief Constable about your behaviour. And another thing, this car is a disgrace; it is muddy and dirty. Is this what I pay my taxes for and what about—'

The old guy keeps yelling at the cop who's looking more and more like he wished he was in bed. After about five minutes of non-stop complaints, he finally has to pause for breath.

'Excuse me,' I say. 'Is it OK if I go to school now – only we've got an exam this morning and I wouldn't like to miss it.'

Not exactly true, I know, but I have to say something or I'll be here till next Tuesday.

'No,' says the old guy.

'What's your name?' asks the cop.

I tell him.

'Right, lad. Keep away from this old man's property in future. Now, get off to school.'

I turn and walk off quickly. Behind me, I can hear the old man yelling, 'Is that all you're going to do, Constable?'

Adults, I despair of them sometimes. I pity

the kid who kicks a football into the old guy's garden. He'll probably sue him for squashing his grass.

I'm just in time to see Macauley disappearing round the corner. I get my bike moving to try to catch him. I was planning to try talking to him today. He's walking fairly fast but I get him in the end.

'Hey,' I say.

He looks up at me and nods. He doesn't say anything.

'You go to St John's,' I say.

'Yeah,' he says.

'What's it like?'

'It's a school.' He's obviously not big on talking.

'Well, yeah, I knew that. I was just wondering what kind of school. My parents are thinking of transferring me.'

'It's the same as all the others,' he says.

'Is it tough?'

He shrugs. His mother must have laid on the never talk to strangers lesson real good. He starts walking faster.

'Is there any bullying there?'

He turns and stares at me like I'm the

dumbest thing on two legs. It's a stupid question. There're thugs in every school.

'Well, thanks for your help,' I say. I feel like a total nothing. Making an idiot of myself in front of an eleven-year-old. My bike gets me away from him fast.

I'm sitting in registration having just received another detention because I was late again. The morons on the back love that. Newman's obviously on one of his get tough binges. New teachers are like that. You never know where you are with them. One week they're a pushover, the next week they're Genghis Khan. Teachers. At least if they did the same thing all the time you'd have some idea how bad you could be.

I'm facing up to the fact that things are going from bad to worse. Two detentions, one warning from the police, one old guy waving a walking stick, not to mention a lousy interview with the alleged victim. I'm about as bad a private investigator as you could find.

I'm trying hard not to think about my conversation with Macauley because it makes me want to squirm, like when your parents tell everybody about something cute you did as a baby and everybody looks at you.

I try and shake off these thoughts. As I look up, the door opens and Katie Pierce walks in with Julie Reece.

'Where have you been?' Newman asks them.

They just ignore him and go and sit down.

'I asked you a question.'

The class quietens down. There's nothing like a good argument to start off the day.

'None of your business,' says Katie Pierce.

Newman looks really angry.

'Don't talk to me like that, young woman. Where have you been?'

Katie Pierce yawns.

Newman walks up to Katie Pierce's desk and stares at her.

'Once more, why are you late?'

'That's not what you asked last time,' says Julie Reece. Katie Pierce laughs and the two of them give each other high fives.

'You're both in late detention,' says Newman. 'Half an hour tonight.'

'No, we're not,' says Katie Pierce. 'The bus was late. It's not our fault.'

'You should be in school on time. Late detention.'

'It's not our fault,' yells Katie Pierce, 'so we're not going.'

Newman starts writing out their detention slip.

'Stop doing that now,' yells Katie Pierce.

'You open your mouth once more and you are in real trouble,' says Newman without looking up.

Katie Pierce shuts up for a second. Even for her, she's pushing her luck.

There's this silence for a bit and everyone starts off talking again. It looks like Katie's been put in her place for once. I've got to give Newman respect for that. Not many teachers manage it.

After a couple of minutes, Katie puts up her hand.

'Sir, I think you're being very unfair.' Her voice is suddenly all sweet. 'It's not our fault we were late. My mother will be very upset when she finds out that I'm in detention for something that wasn't my fault.'

Katie throws in her ace. Her dreaded mother is guaranteed to scare every teacher in the world. Sometimes I wish I had a mother like that rather than one who says, 'If the teacher says you were messing about the teacher must be right,' like mine does.

Newman stares at Katie. This is crunch time and everybody in the class knows it. We've seen it before. If he crumbles in front of the threat of Katie's mother, she'll run rings round him for ever.

'Tell her to come in and see me. I'll be happy to discuss it with her.'

Round one to Newman. Katie looks like she can't believe it. I'm beginning to like him. You can see people round the class looking at each other and thinking maybe he's going to make the grade after all.

The thing about my class is that they give teachers grief. The morons at the back are always pinching each others' pencils and kicking one another and throwing stuff across the classroom and girls like Katie or Julie get their kicks mouthing off to the teacher about how rubbish he is. Then the teacher gets mad and is horrible to the whole class and then the whole class is horrible back to him and half the lessons turn into all-out war. I just watch most of it go off. I'm not really interested in it. I used to be but winding teachers up gets boring after a while, every lesson is just shouting. The trouble is that nobody ever learns anything. That's OK for the morons at the back who don't care but it's lousy for someone like Umair who wants to be a lawyer. I mean, when he's in court and he gets confused about something, what can he say, 'I'm sorry, Judge, but the morons at the back were throwing pencils at me the day we did that'?

The thing is the only person who can stop it is a teacher. If Umair stood up and said, 'Shut up, you lot, I want to learn something,' he'd be a crawler for the rest of his life.

Suddenly, Newman yells out, 'Mr Sharp.' He's got this big smirk on his face so I must be in trouble. I begin to dislike him again.

'I see you failed to attend your detention, yesterday. Why?'

The class gave a big 'Aaaah' when he says that as if I'd just been arrested for murder or something. I tell him I forgot. It's such a lousy excuse I feel embarrassed saying it. The morons at the back get really excited.

'You can't let him get away with that, sir.'

'I said "I forgot" last week and you said it wasn't good enough.'

'He didn't forget.'

I thought kids were supposed to be on the kid's side.

'Give him another detention, sir.'

'Give him another two detentions.'

'Send him to Walton.'

'Get him suspended.'

I saw this movie once, set in ancient Rome. These two gladiators would fight each other in this massive stadium and when one guy won he would point his sword against the heart of the loser. Then he would turn round to the crowd and ask them whether he should kill him or not. The crowd would put their thumbs up if they wanted the guy to live and their thumbs down if they wanted him to die. I feel like the loser did when he saw all the crowd's thumbs going down.

'Thank you, everybody,' says Newman, 'but I think I can decide Mickey's punishment without assistance. I'm the teacher and I'm in charge.'

Katie Pierce comes out with this big snort

when he says that. She means him to hear but he just ignores her.

'Mickey, you can add half an hour on to tonight's detention because you missed last night's. Now you'll have an hour tonight to practise improving your memory skills and half an hour on Monday.'

The class give him a big cheer for that.

This is getting out of hand. If I'm going to have any chance of getting anywhere in this case, I can't afford to waste my life in detention.

I decide to get out of it. All I have to do is find a flaw in the system. What happens is this. The teachers put the late-detention slips in a box in the school office. Then, at the end of the day, the deputy head takes the box with all the names on it to the late-detention room to check everybody's there. If you don't turn up, the slip gets a cross on it and they double it, and if you miss that one they phone your parents. My dad goes in for the big perform-ances when he hears I'm in trouble at school. No pocket money, no going out, no TV – the works. I can do without that right now. What

I have to do is get the slip out of the box before the end of school. It shouldn't be too hard.

I wait until after break to make sure Mr Newman's had time to get the slip into the box.

Then, about ten minutes into period three when Miss Hardy's getting all flushed because some kid's asking her what the French is for 'I love you', I stick my hand up and get a note to go to the toilet. They don't like letting you out but if you get them at the right time then they've said 'yes' before they realize what you've asked them.

Once you've got a note you can go anywhere. I'm straight down to the school office.

All I've got to do now is get the school secretary out of there but that's going to be tougher. She really hates moving. She's about sixty, she sits in her office all day, eating chocolates, smoking cigarettes and pretending to type.

So, I tap on her little window. She looks over at me with this look which says she's really busy which is garbage because all she's doing is choosing between an orange cream and a strawberry cup. She sighs and opens the window.

'Yes.'

She's a real charmer. I try to look as innocent as possible.

'Miss, I wanted to tell you that I was just in the boys' toilets by the art block and there were some boys in there that aren't from our school.'

'How do you know?'

'They're too old.'

'Why are you telling me? Why not tell a teacher?'

She has a point there but I'm ready for her.

'I went to Mr Walton's office but he's not there.'

'What can I do?' She's really angry.

'Dunno, miss. I'll go back and see if they're still there.'

And I run off leaving her with a problem.

I know what she'll do. She'll curse me for picking on her to tell and then she'll try to forget about it. But she'll be worried in case they do something and it comes out that she knew about them. Strangers in the school is a big deal in our school. The head gets all red in the face at assembly and threatens to expel anyone who talks to them. He's all mouth. The only thing he can expel is air.

Sure enough two minutes later she's waddling off to the staff room to find some teacher to check it out. I wait till she's out of sight, nip in the door, find the box, grab my slips and run off back to class. No worries.

I feel a bit more cheerful after getting out of the detentions. There's nothing like undermining the system for getting the adrenalin going. I surprise myself a bit by answering a question in French. I get it wrong but then I always do. If I'd got it right, I'd have started worrying.

So, by the end of the day I'm free to slip off and tail Macauley again. I have to bunk another class but the Friday afternoon in our school is normally given over to bad behaviour anyway. I can miss one week of watching our Music teacher's confidence being destroyed.

Three fifteen and there I am waiting outside St John's. To avoid police attention I don't lean against any walls. You never know when an old guy might be watching.

Schools are always dangerous places on

Fridays. You keep kids in a school for five days and they get bored. They feel like the fizz in a bottle of Coke just waiting to be opened. Friday afternoon when the bell goes is the cap being twisted. Twist the cap and the fizz usually bubbles up for a couple of seconds and then calms down. Every now and then though, it explodes all over you. That's why teachers look nervous on Friday afternoons – they're just waiting to see if the fizz explodes.

It's looking like one of those dangerous afternoons here at St John's. There're some older kids hanging about the school looking mean. They probably used to go there. I can never work out why older kids do that. They probably couldn't wait to get out of the place and now they're out, all they do is hang around acting tough. Mind you, I keep out of their way because they're acting tough pretty convincingly.

So, the bell goes and the kids start coming out. There's a few teachers there too, trying to herd the kids out of the gate like they're sheep or something. There's a bang like someone set a fire cracker off and some cheering but the teachers keep them moving.

Then, suddenly, there's a fight in the playground. You can tell it's a fight straight off because all the kids go charging towards it to form a big circle around it, yelling like crazy. The teachers are in there fast though. This big bald guy's battling his way through the crowd. This woman comes over too and the circle starts splitting up. Nobody wants to get caught at the scene of the crime. Then the bald guy comes out holding two kids. They're only about twelve. I always feel sorry for fighters when they get caught, especially when they're little; they always look so pathetic hanging from the teacher's arms.

And then just while I'm watching the fighters being dragged back into school I catch sight of Macauley. He's walking his old bored determined walk, as ever, but there's something different about him. He's got blood pouring from his nose.

I let him get out of sight of the school and then I catch him up.

'Hey,' I say, for the second time that day.

He doesn't answer. Still, you don't normally want to start making new friends straight after being beaten up.

'We were talking this morning, you remember?'

He puts his head down and walks faster.

'Hey, I just want to be friendly.' This is terrible. I'm starting to sound like a dirty old man. 'Look. What happened? I thought you said St John's wasn't tough.'

He hadn't said that but I'm prepared to try anything. He still isn't biting though. He just keeps on walking. Every now and then a drop of blood falls from his nose on to the pavement.

'Hey, come on, what happened to you?'

He turns round and stares at me just like this morning. From the look on his face you can tell we aren't ever going to be friends.

'Go away.'

He turns round and runs towards his house. I watch him disappear into the distance, his bag banging against his side all the way down the road.

I'm not going to get anything out of him in that state. So, I wheel my bike around and head for home. I need a Coke.

*   *   *

I'm sitting in the shed trying to think out what I've discovered. It's not much. I know someone at school is bullying Macauley Stone. To find this out has cost me two bunked classes, two detentions (unattended), one warning from the police and one old guy waving a walking stick. On top of that, Macauley won't talk to me and I am no nearer finding out who is bullying him. Why couldn't my first case be easier? Like a murder or something.

I'm chewing over what to do next when the door opens and Madeleine walks in. She looks like someone just lit a fire inside her. She's angry.

'What kind of detective do you call yourself?' she starts off. 'I have just seen my brother's face and it is covered in blood. You were supposed to stop this kind of thing and instead it's getting worse. Congratulations.'

I don't say anything. She has plenty more complaining to do before she's finished.

'Why did I bring this job to you? You're obviously incapable of living up to your advert. My brother is in danger and you are sitting here drinking Coke. Well, what do you have to say for yourself?'

She would make a great teacher.

I shrug and say that these things take time. It doesn't convince her.

'While you are taking all this time, my brother is being bullied. I want you to sort it out and I want you to sort it out quickly. Understand?'

I just stare at her but I guess she figures she's made her point because she stands up and storms out without any farewells. She slams the door. The shed shakes.

I wonder if I look like a punch bag. Everybody I meet seems to want to take a shot at me.

I go into dinner with my family. For once, I'm glad to see them. At least they mainly criticize each other.

CHAPTER FOUR

When I wake up the next morning things don't seem so bad. After dinner last night I sat in the shed trying to work out what to do. How was I going to find out who was bullying Macauley? I thought about it and thought about it. Thinking can be really tough when you try to do it for a long time. I didn't come up with anything and in the end I gave up and went to bed. And then just when I was about to go to sleep the answer flashed into my mind. I wrote it down just in case I forgot it.

And there's the piece of paper by my bed with 'Undercover' written on it.

My father reckons that you can go anywhere in a hospital if you wear a white coat and that you can wander all round the Houses of Parliament if you've got a smart suit and some important looking papers in your hand. On this evidence, if you've got a clear complexion and a stupid grin you can probably present children's TV. All you need to get into a school is the right uniform.

St John's uniform seemed fairly standard stuff. Having spent two afternoons there I'm pretty sure of what I need: grey v-necked jumper, white shirt, red-and-white striped tie, grey trousers and black shoes. I've got the shirt, the trousers and the shoes. I need the tie and the jumper. Washing lines seem a good place to start.

Two hours later, I'm not so sure. When I was younger I remember that everyone seemed to use washing lines. They were good things to throw soil at. Now everybody uses dryers. They stink a bit but nobody throws soil at them.

I'm going to have to get the uniform from somewhere else. What do people do with old school ties? I'd probably burn mine but everybody can't do that. They throw them out. Where do people throw old clothes out to? Charity shops.

So, I set off to hit the charity shops. Cancer Relief's no use; Oxfam's equally hopeless. Save the Children which I thought might be big on school uniforms has nothing either. I'm fast getting fed up with charity shops. They all seem the same, old ladies selling books that nobody will ever read and clothes that nobody will ever wear.

Cafod's better though. There, on a rack at the back, are two St John's ties. I buy the one which smells the least bad. The old woman wants a pound for it. I tell her my family are very poor and I can only afford 50p but she won't budge. For someone who's supposed to be charitable she drives a hard bargain. I give in and hand over the cash. I make sure she gives me a receipt though. How else am I going to get my expenses back from Madeleine?

Now all I need is the jumper. A grey V-necked jumper's exactly the sort of thing that David would have. David lives three doors down from me and he's the only kid I know who chooses clothes that look more like school uniform than school uniform does. I stop off at home on my way back to grab a Coke thinking that I'll skip over to David's later on. Stopping off at home is a mistake.

I'm just leaving the kitchen when my mother catches me.

'Mickey,' she says, 'your grandmother's here. Go in and talk to her.'

This is terrible news. I try to wriggle out of it.

'I've got to go over to David's. He's got some stuff I need for school. I'll be back soon. I'll see her then.'

I don't think there is much chance it's going to work. My mother knows she won't see me again for hours.

'Go in there now and talk to her.'

'I really would like to but this stuff is important.'

'Now. You know you're her favourite.'

There's this myth in our family that my grandmother likes me. Truth is, she doesn't like me at all, she likes criticizing people and I'm her favourite because she can find most wrong with me. It really cheers her up.

I walk in and say hello.

She tells me my hair's too long, my clothes are horrid and asks me when I last had a bath. It's her way of saying hello.

I tell her that I can't remember the last time

I had a bath. I tell her I have showers.

She looks really happy when I tell her that. She tells me showers don't work properly. She says I must have at least two baths a week.

I don't say anything.

She tells me to work harder at school, to help my mother more in the house and to make sure I say my prayers every night.

I nod and say I've got to go.

She tells me to take more exercise, watch less TV and join the boy scouts.

I leave the room. She doesn't even give you money like a proper grandparent.

I sneak out the front door so my mother won't catch me and send me back in to my dear grandmother. If you're really unlucky you can get stuck playing cards with her. It can go on for hours.

I go over to David's. His dad tells me he's up in the attic with his trains. This is no surprise. David lives for his trains; he's been collecting them since he was a kid. The track goes all the way round his attic about four times. I've never seen the appeal myself.

I climb up the stairs and stick my head into the attic.

'Hi,' I say.

'Not now,' he replies without looking at me. 'My Inter City Pullman's just got derailed. There could be casualties.'

'I'm in no hurry,' I tell him and pull myself fully into the attic.

Never expect hospitality from a train nut.

I try to ignore the fact that he's started wearing a cap on his head, he's got a whistle dangling round his neck and a green flag in his hand. However badly I need a favour I'm not going to be able to come up with anything polite to say about this.

He does a bit of messing about with his trains and he shakes his head a lot. He's the only person I know who could hear of a train crash in which a whole load of people are injured and feel sorry for the train.

Finally, everything seems to start running again and he looks a bit more relaxed.

'It's looking good,' I try.

He shakes his head.

'That accident's put my whole daily time-table behind. There'll have to be an inquiry.'

I get in my question fast.

'Have you got a grey V-necked jumper?'

'I don't know.'

'Can you find out?'

'Try my room.'

I climb down and go to his room. It's covered with pictures of trains. Even his duvet cover's got trains on. There's two old British Rail timetables on his bedside table. I bet he doesn't find it too hard to get to sleep. I rifle through his cupboard and find three grey V-necked jumpers. Three. He's got less imagination than I suspected. I try them on and take the one that fits best.

I head back up to the attic. David's still playing. But he actually notices me this time.

'You'll be pleased to know that the inquiry exonerated me. A points failure. No question of human error whatsoever.'

'That was quick.'

'I hope you're not suggesting a cover-up.'

'No way. I have absolute faith in the decision.'

'Did you find a jumper?'

'Yeah. Can I borrow it?'

'Depends.'

'On what?'

'On whether I can borrow you.'

'Borrow me?'

'There's an auction of old British Rail memorabilia tomorrow. I need someone to come and help me carry home the things I'm going to buy.'

'Oh.'

'You'll enjoy it. It will show you a whole new world.'

I don't want to see a whole new world but I don't have any choice. I say I'll meet him outside my house at ten.

The next day is one of the worst I'll ever spend. Trains, trains and more trains. David comes home a happy man. I come home determined to use the bus.

To pass the time I ask him how he thinks you stop bullies from bullying other people. You know what he says, 'Buy them a train set.' David is never going to be much help when it comes to the difficult questions.

I'm fed up by the time I get home. David had bought loads of stuff and I've had to carry it. He saves up all his pocket money for six months and then spends it all at once on train stuff. Then when he's finished buying stuff, he has to go round talking to loads of other people about trains. That's the thing about train fanatics. You think there can't be many more of them but then you go to some auction like this and you find out that there are hundreds and thousands of them and they're all as mad as each other. David, of course, loves every minute of it and it is impossible to get him to leave. In the end, I have to threaten to dump all the stuff he's bought and go home without him. That gets him moving.

When I get back to my house it's time for dinner. My mum makes this big Sunday roast and my grandmother comes over. When you add my grandmother to my family the arguments get even worse.

Anyway, we are all getting ready to start eating when my dad comes in.

'Right,' he says, 'I've decided that there will be some changes around here.'

My mother looks at him weirdly but he doesn't seem to notice.

'I have been thinking about us,' he goes on, 'and I have decided that we must become more of a family. We never seem to do anything together any more. Apart from at meal times, we never seem to see each other.'

The reason we don't spend any time together outside meal times is because of what happens at meal times. We fight.

'I think that from next week we should all start going to church together. Religion will make us more of a family,' he says.

This piece of news does not go down too well with me and I can see from my mother's face that she isn't too happy. I don't like church. It's boring. Years ago, we used to go to church every Sunday but then we stopped. Now we only go at Christmas because my mother likes the carols. I don't mind going then because I figure that if you're getting presents and stuff you've got to do something boring to earn them.

Nobody says anything though because my dad's in one of his moods. It's as if he's really desperate for an argument and so he comes out with some idea that everybody hates so that they'll argue with him about it and then he can shout at them. I used to fall for it last year and start arguing with him but it's point-less arguing with my father because even if I win he can still send me to my room for being cheeky.

But it seems like nobody is in the mood for an argument because nobody says anything. Finally, my grandmother says, 'I think that's a very good idea. Perhaps if we are being more religious someone should say a blessing over the food before we start.'

She looks at me when she says this because my mouth is already full of food. I put my knife and fork down.

My dad mumbles something about thanking God for the food we've got and then we start eating. I don't know why we're thanking God – it's my mum who earned the money to pay for it.

Nobody says anything for the whole meal. I think I preferred the fighting.

Afterwards, I slip off down to the shed to avoid my grandmother. I've been there about ten minutes just listening to some tapes when there's a knock on the door.

It's my sister.

This is really odd because she hardly ever comes down here. We don't talk much these days. She's two and a half years older than me which she always tells me whenever we have an argument. She seems to think that because she's older than me that means she's right. That's stupid if you ask me. If you saw politicians on the news shouting, 'I'm right because I'm older than you are,' nobody would believe them so why should I believe her? I said that to her once and she said, 'Mickey, you don't understand. I'm seventeen and I have much more experience of life than you have.' That's rubbish too. The only thing that she's done that I haven't is go camping in Wales for a week with her friends.

She comes in and kind of wanders around. You can tell she wants to say something but she doesn't seem to know how to come out with it. I give her a bit of time.

It's funny how we stopped hanging round together. When we were younger we used to play all kinds of stuff. Then, when she got to be about twelve, she stopped wanting to do anything which involved running around. She hung around her bedroom and messed about with make-up and dressing up in different clothes. She didn't really know what she was doing with lipstick and stuff in those days. She used to come out of her room looking like a panda with these big blue circles round her eyes. She's got better at it since then. And her friends used to come round and whenever they saw me they all started laughing or going, 'Aaah look, it's Karen's little brother. Isn't he cute?' I'm not big on people calling me cute and so I made sure I kept out of their way. Then, before I knew it, I found out that we weren't friends any more. We argue sometimes these days because she's always so moody but mostly we just keep out of each other's way.

Finally, she comes out with her question.

'Do you think Dad's OK?'

'I don't know,' I say. 'He seems to be getting weirder.'

I don't know what to say about my dad any more. I don't like to think about him much really.

'He's given up looking for a job,' she says.

'Oh,' I say.

There's a pause and then she turns round

and heads for the door. It doesn't look like it's going to turn out to be much of a conversation. She opens the door, then she seems to change her mind and shuts it again.

'Mickey,' she says. 'Can I ask you a question?'

'Sure,' I say.

'You won't mention it to anyone?'

I shake my head.

She looks down at the floor. 'Do you think I'm fat?'

I was expecting something really big after all that build up and it's only that. It's a really dumb question as well. My sister is one of the skinniest girls I know. She's always going on diets and stuff that they tell you about in these magazines. And she hardly ever eats much. I'd be starving if I ate as little as she does. My mum's always going on about it but my sister says she's got a really small appetite.

'No,' I say. 'Not at all.'

'Really,' she says. 'Not even like this.'

She turns round so I can see her sideways.

She does it really nervously like she's suddenly going to look incredibly fat like you do in those weird mirrors at fairs. She still looks thin.

'No,' I say. 'You're not fat. You're really thin.'

'I don't know,' she says. 'Sometimes I think that if I could just get rid of a few pounds off my bum.'

I look away. It's not nice hearing your sister talk about her bum. I hope I'm not going to have to listen to a load of talk about diets. My sister and her friends are always going on about how heavy they are like it's the only thing that matters in the world. They talk about supermodels and they say, 'They're so thin,' like they've done something amazing. Just for being thin. It's not like they've saved the universe or understood the past tense in French.

'Would you do me a favour, Mickey?' she says.

I nod. I've got nothing better to do. I just hope it's nothing to do with calories.

'Will you take some photos of me? I

want to practise looking right.'

So, with Dad's camera I spend the next hour taking some photos of her. It's OK. At first, she's really serious telling me how she wants to look and all that but after a while she calms down and just lets me try my best. I haven't taken many pictures before but I think I've started to get the hang of it.

In the end, we're just messing about taking silly pictures in the garden. It takes my mind off things. I even let her take a couple of shots of me and I'm not really too keen on having my picture taken. I think it's because when we were younger and my dad used to take all these photos he'd always be yelling, 'Smile, smile,' and he wouldn't press the button until you had a smile on your face so wide that you thought your face was going to break. Then, when the photos came out, I'd look like a grinning idiot. Take a look at my father's albums. You'd think our whole family never did anything but smile all the time.

I make sure that on one of the photos I look serious. At least then there will be one picture of me in the world where I don't look like a moron.

We take a whole film in the end. I take it out and Karen gets a new film out but she decides not to use it.

'You have it,' she says to me. 'Thanks for doing me a favour.'

'What about Dad?' I say. 'It's his camera.'

'He never uses it any more,' she says.

She's right. He hasn't taken any pictures for ages.

She hands the film and the camera over to me and heads off back inside. She turns round when she reaches the back door.

'It might be useful,' she says. 'I hear you're a detective these days.'

I'm really surprised when she says that. I didn't think anybody in my family knew. I didn't tell them because I was pretty certain they wouldn't be interested.

The trouble is it reminds me about tomorrow. If I'm going to be any good as a detective, tomorrow's when I'm going to have to prove it. Going undercover seemed a great idea on Saturday morning. But now that I'm really going to have to do it, I'm not sure. It seems like there are a lot of things which could go wrong.

CHAPTER FIVE

Monday morning and it's back to school, but just for a change, I'm off to a different one. I stuff my toast down, pick up my bulging school bag and say goodbye to my mother. She looks at me oddly. Maybe I don't usually say goodbye. I march down our street an upright pupil of Hanford High. Ten minutes later, after a small detour to some waste ground, I'm walking down the street as a well-dressed pupil of St John's. My idea is to get into the school, hide in the toilets during lessons and follow Macauley round at break and lunch to see who's giving him grief. It feels foolproof to me. I've left my bike at home because I don't know how safe it'll be at St John's. I've let one of the tyres down so I can say that it's got a puncture if my parents start asking awkward questions.

I get to St John's just before the bell goes and hang around in the yard looking like every kid does on a Monday morning – depressed. Nobody's very interested in anybody else at this time so I don't get any unwanted attention. I see Macauley walk through the gates about five minutes after me. I look away. I don't want him to know I'm there.

The bell goes and the kids start walking into the school. I follow the crowd and start trying to spot the toilets. In about three minutes the corridors will be deserted with all the kids in their classrooms. I'll need somewhere to hide.

A minute goes past. I can't see any sign of them. I start walking down the corridors faster. I still can't see them. Another minute goes past. Already the corridors are thinning out, with kids going into their classrooms. Pretty soon I'm going to be out here on my own. I start moving really fast but the trouble is that it's like being a new kid at school all over again – it's real easy to get lost. I might be going round in circles, going down the same corridors all the time. Almost all the kids are in class by now and I still don't have anywhere to go. In about another ten seconds I'm going to have to answer some difficult questions. I turn down one last corridor. I'm pretty much running now. I see a red door with 'BOYS' written on it. Never have I been happier to see a toilet. I slow down and look round to see if there's any teachers watching. All clear. I push the door. It's locked.

I try it again in the hope that there might be a miracle. It's still locked. I turn round. The corridor is deserted. I start walking back down it. My only hope is to keep moving, to look like I know where I'm going. I turn round a corner. I'm really lost now. Maybe there's another toilet. I'm desperate.

'You, boy.'

A booming voice comes from behind me. I keep walking, hoping it's not me he's after.

'Don't you dare walk away when a teacher is addressing you.'

It is me. I stop and turn round. There's a huge teacher with a beard like a dodgy Father Christmas standing at the other end of the corridor.

'Do you know what time it is?' he yells. 'You should be in class by now.' I look down at the floor.

'Don't dawdle, boy. You've wasted enough

time as it is. Get to class. I hope you get a detention.'

I should phone the Guinness Book of World Records. I'll be the only kid to have detentions at two schools at the same time.

I turn back around and walk down the corridor. If I can get round the corner I can run. But things aren't going to be that easy. The corridor is a dead end.

I figure I don't have too many options. I can't turn back with the teacher behind me and I can't walk through walls. I take a deep breath and walk into the nearest classroom.

There's a teacher sitting at the desk marking the register. He looks up when I walk in.

'Ever heard of knocking?' he says.

My heart's banging away inside me. I'm not really concentrating and I don't get what he says.

'What?'

'I asked you if you'd ever heard of knocking. It's an ancient and polite tradition which seems to be fast fading from the behaviour of the younger members of our society. Knocking on a door before opening it, you remember?'

He looks at me. I guess I must have seemed a bit dumb to him because he just shakes his head and says, 'Never mind. What do you want?'

I don't know what to say so I don't say anything. The class start laughing. I feel great.

'Shall I say it slower? What . . . do . . . you . . . want?'

He's one of those sarcastic teachers. The class start laughing louder. I've got to say something. I look round and say the first thing I see, 'Chalk.'

He looks confused, 'What?'

'Sir says can he borrow some chalk.'

He looks at me suspiciously. I try to look stupid and innocent at the same time. It's my only chance. He leans over and picks up a stick of a chalk and hands it to me.

'There you go. Next time knock when you're going into a classroom.'

I take the chalk and walk out of the class praying that the big teacher has gone. I walk into the corridor. It's empty.

I feel like I've just been on a ten mile cross country run. My heart is pounding. I need to get out of sight. I start walking back the way

I came. I don't know where I'm going but I've got to go somewhere. As I walk past the toilets I give the door a kick for old times' sake. The door moves. I push it. It opens. Maybe they unlock them as soon as all the kids are stuck in class and can't use them. Typical. They probably lock it again before break. I get into a cubicle real fast, and slam the door shut. Sanctuary.

So now I'm back with my plan and I settle down to wait. It'll probably be an hour till break so I've got some time to kill. I check out the graffiti. It's mainly your standard stuff. Swear words, football teams and sex. I've never been into graffiti. I don't see the point. Every kid at school knows all the swear words, so who are you impressing by writing them on the wall? Especially when half the kids can't even spell the words they're writing. Maybe teachers should teach you how to spell swear words. After all, half the kids at school use them more often than anything else.

Football teams just lead to arguments. Some kid writes 'Spurs' on the wall. Then some other kid comes along and writes 'are rubbish' underneath. Then some other kid writes 'but not as bad as Chelsea' below that. Then some other kid comes along and crosses out 'Chelsea' and puts in 'Arsenal'. Then another kid comes along and sticks a 'NOT!' at the end. And finally a kid comes along and crosses out the 'Spurs' and writes in 'Liverpool'. It's not even as though they're getting their message across.

Sex is the weirdest of all though. Some kids write their name and their girlfriend's name on a toilet door. In this toilet you've got a 'Cornell & Carly' and a 'Luke 4 Maria'. It's sad. All you do is make sure that all the kids think of you going out together when they're doing their business. Why do people want that? I don't know. If a girl ever wrote my name in a toilet it would be the end. Not that you'd ever find out though.

Then there's the graffiti you can't work out. Most of these are tags. A tag is a kid's graffiti name. Loads of kids have them. A kid in my class called Darren Watson signs himself Dr Zoom all over the school. I suppose he thinks it makes him more interesting but it doesn't. He does it in real fancy letters so it's really hard to read. He's really dedicated though and his tags are everywhere. The head went mad about it. He said that if he found out who Dr Zoom was he'd expel him. Like I said before, our head's always threatening to chuck people out of school. I reckon he'd be happy running a school without any kids, he seems to hate us all so much. They got Darren in the end though, he'd been practising his tag at the back of his Maths book. They didn't chuck him out but he spent a week scrubbing and repainting the walls. Everyone calls him the Caretaker now. He's got no respect.

There's also this big bit of graffiti on one side of the cubicle I'm in. It says, 'IT PAYS TO PAY THE PROFESSIONALS.' I can't work it out at all.

Nothing much happens while I'm locked in the toilets. You can hear kids come in and out now and then. I just keep the door locked and wait. Whenever a kid comes in I stick my feet up in the air so they won't be able to see there's anybody there if they look under the door. I don't know why anybody would look under a toilet door but I'm playing it safe.

Actually, not many kids come in. It's not

like Hanford High where there's always at least five kids in the toilets when there's lessons on. Maybe it's a better school than Hanford. Mind you, that wouldn't be hard. I saw this thing on the news once. There was this grey guy with glasses going on about inspecting schools and how inspectors had to work really hard to find out whether a school was good or not. I reckon that's rubbish. To find out how good a school is just spend a few hours in the toilets. If loads of kids are coming in all the time, it's probably terrible. If nobody comes in, it's probably good. That's not hard, is it?

Whichever way you look at it spending two hours in a toilet is not really much fun. I figure I should charge extra for working in antisocial conditions. After I've read the graffiti about a thousand times, the bell goes for break. I get out of the toilet and head off to look for Macauley.

I'd forgotten how tough it is to get round a school when you don't know it. I can't see Macauley anywhere and I don't want to tip him off that I'm looking for him by asking some little kid. I spend ten minutes wandering around the school but I still can't spot him. I decide that instead of going round the school maybe if I stand still he'll come past me. It's easier on the feet. I find this post on the far side of the yard with a good view of lots of kids and lean against it. Two minutes later I'm still trying to pick him out when somebody taps me on the shoulder. I turn round, praying it's not a teacher. It's not. It's a kid and he's got some friends with him.

'Hello,' says the kid.

He's about the same size as me but a bit older. He's one of those guys who get over-excited when they get the first few hairs on their top lips and try to turn it into a moustache. I'm pretty sure he'd tell you it was a moustache if you asked him. I'd describe it as a few hairs. However, his friends, who are standing right behind, are on the big side so I decide not to mention it.

'Hi,' I say.

'Allow me to introduce myself,' he says with a big smile. 'My name is Anthony. These are my friends Nico and Giovanni.'

I nod to the two lumps behind him.

'I have not seen you here before,' he continues.

'Oh,' I say. I don't see any reason to help him out.

'You are new then?'

I nod.

'I thought so. I make a special effort to welcome all the new boys to the school. I think it is so important to create a sense of community in the school, don't you agree?' His smile gets even wider.

'I'm sure your mother's very proud of you,' I say smiling back.

For a second his smile disappears.

'We do not need to talk of my mother,' he says.

'She's *your* mother,' I agree.

'Yes,' he replies, 'she is. But I want to talk to you about the school.'

'Fire away,' I tell him.

He keeps his smile on his face though you can tell that it's a bit of an effort.

'St John's is a very good school,' he says. 'Would you not say so, Nico?'

Nico manages to say, 'yes', but he has to put a lot of thought into it.

'However,' Anthony continues, 'it does have a problem. There are some violent, dangerous boys in this school. These boys tend to pick on small boys or new boys like yourself. It is very wrong of them but these boys do not have a highly developed sense of morality. They tend to think with their fists. Some of the boys who have come up against them have been badly injured.'

He pauses as though he wants me to say something. I keep silent. I'm pretty sure what's coming next.

'However, myself and Nico and Giovanni and some of our associates have decided to stop these beatings, the violence of which upsets us so much. We believe very strongly in good behaviour.'

'Your mother obviously brought you up well,' I say.

Anthony grits his teeth.

'We do not need to speak of my mother.'

'Oh. I forgot,' I tell him.

'We have organized into a group to protect small boys and new boys like yourself from these attacks.'

'What a noble idea,' I tell him.

'So you will be able to walk safely about St John's.'

'That's very kind of you,' I pat Anthony on the shoulder. He grits his teeth even harder than before.

'However,' he says, removing my arm, 'all this protection cannot be given free. Nico and Giovanni and many others are working hard all the time to keep you safe. It is only fair that they receive some kind of reward for their efforts.'

'Nico and Giovanni look so kind that I'm sure that doing good is all the reward they need,' I say. Nico and Giovanni look about as kind as King Kong and his big brother.

'How I wish that were so,' says Anthony, 'but sadly there are many expenses which crop up when you are protecting the innocent. I'm sure you understand. Perhaps you will bring a contribution towards their expenses to school tomorrow. I will see that it goes to the right place.'

Then, while smiling his big smile, Anthony pats me on the cheek and the three of them walk off across the yard.

So now I'm being bullied. Great.

The bell rings.

I wander back into the school and duck into the toilet. I have about an hour and a half to sit and wait for lunch. I'm going to have to make sure I manage to find Macauley this time or the day will be a complete waste.

One thing is certain. Anthony and his boys have a fairly professional operation going here. It took them only fifteen minutes to spot a new boy and tell him the facts of life at St John's. They know what they're doing. With an operation as good as that it's likely that they're behind what's happening to Macauley Stone. Then again, there's an awful lot of nutters walking round most schools and it could be someone else. I'm going to have to catch them in the act and I'm going to have to do it soon. Teachers are dumb but just wearing a uniform isn't going to fool them for ever.

Anybody who's done Geography on a regular basis for three years has a good training in putting up with being bored but the next two hours in the toilet really stretch even my ability. I make sure it's a different cubicle to add variety but it doesn't do much good. I try not to look at my watch because it seems to go slower every time I look. I try to play 'I spy' with myself but it's tough getting it wrong when you already know what's been spied. In the end I settle on thinking about Madeleine. It passes the time quicker than anything else.

Finally the bell goes and kids start heading out for lunch. It's easy to find Macauley this time. All you do is follow the stream of kids heading towards the dinner hall. Nothing gets kids moving like food. There's an old story which some teacher read to us in primary school about this guy who played magic music on a pipe and because this music was so amazing all the kids in the town followed him and he led them to the river and they drowned or something. I don't buy that. What kid do you know that would follow a flute player? If the guy had walked off with a whole load of burgers and chips then the kids would have followed him all right.

So, I get to the dinner hall and they're letting the young kids in first and about halfway down the queue I spot Macauley. I try and keep out of sight while keeping an eye on him.

He's his old boring self. He's not saying much and he's looking as serious as ever. I'm finding it very tough to believe Madeleine that he was once the most wonderful little brother in the world. Still, if he was, he sure has changed.

I hang around outside the dinner hall waiting for him to come out. This dinner lady gives me a few odd stares but she doesn't say anything. Dinner ladies don't normally bother much unless you're actually in the process of burning the school down. Then they might tell you to calm down a bit.

Macauley appears with this other kid, the one he walked home with when I followed him last week, and sets off round the back of the school. I hold back but keep him in sight. At the back of the school they've got a big field and the two of them start walking right across it to the far corner. It's tough to follow them without standing out but then again I can see them from quite a distance so I don't need to get too close. I sit down and get a book out of my bag to make it look like I'm doing something while I keep an eye on them.

They're not doing much so I have a glance round the field. It's the usual stuff going on. About ten games of football all banging into each other. One game's going across another game and you'd bet that it would cause chaos but somehow they manage to avoid each other most of the time. There're some other kids just sitting in groups on the grass and over behind what I think is the gym I can see a small group who are smoking their guts out. You can always tell a group of kids smoking. They're all bunched close together and they all look shifty.

There's a couple of dinner ladies having a gossip over by one entrance to the school and a few little kids just running around for no reason. Little kids do that; I've no idea why.

That's about it so I turn back to check out Macauley and mate. They're still hidden over in the corner of the field not doing much. Nothing is happening today. I am getting very bored.

I've been lying like that for a bit when I hear somebody. I glance over my shoulder and register two more kids heading straight for me. For a kid on his first day I'm certainly managing to meet people.

'All right,' says one kid.

I nod.

'How are you doing?' he continues.

'I'm doing good,' I tell him.

'My name's Darren,' says the first one.

'And my name's Wayne,' says the other guy.

They are difficult to tell apart. I think Wayne's slightly uglier but they could both win prizes.

'You're the. . .' begins Darren

'New guy,' finishes off Wayne.

I nod again.

'We've come to tell you about . . .' starts Darren.

'The school,' ends Wayne.

I smile.

'Go ahead,' I tell them.

'This school,' says Darren, 'is a very. . .'

'Good school,' adds Wayne.

'But,' continues Darren, 'it does have some. . .'

'Problems,' says Wayne.

There is a French phrase which sums up what is happening to me now but I can't remember what it is. Serves me right for not paying any attention in class. It's something to do with hearing or seeing something that you've already heard before. I'm getting it now.

'These problems,' Darren informs me, 'are to do with some boys in the school who are. . .'

'Violent,' says Wayne who looks like he's just used his favourite word.

I have to stop them. Listening to Darren and Wayne talk is like watching a game of tennis. I tell them that I've already been treated to the 'problems at St John's' speech. They both look a little glum when I tell them.

'Who spoke to you?' says Darren. I'm really impressed; he's finished a sentence all by himself.

'Anthony.'

'Anthony,' Wayne repeats.

'You got it,' I compliment him.

'Anthony's fine,' says Darren, but he doesn't look too happy. 'So you know the score?'

'Yeah,' I says.

'Right,' he says. 'I've got more customers to see.'

'Hey, before you go, can I ask you a question?'

'What?' says Wayne. I start to wonder whether Wayne has a medical problem that means he can't say more than two words together.

'If I pay Anthony, is that the same as paying you, or do I have to pay you as well? It sounds like this could start getting expensive.'

'Anthony spoke to you first, you pay him,' says Darren.

'Then you're safe,' says Wayne. I was wrong. Three whole words.

'So you and Anthony are in the same gang,' I ask.

'Let's say we have an . . .' Darren searches for the right word.

'Arrangement,' Wayne supplies it for him.

'You're partners, then?' I suggest.

'You ask too many questions,' says Darren.

'Just make sure you pay Anthony tomorrow,' says Wayne, 'or things could get nasty.'

Wayne's really coming out of his shell. I reckon he was just shy in front of strangers but once he knows you well enough to threaten you, there's no stopping him.

'We have other calls to make,' says Darren. 'Let's go.'

They walk past me and on towards the far corner. It doesn't take a great detective to work out that the object of their next call is going to be Macauley.

I watch Darren and Wayne lumber over towards Macauley and his friend. The little kids must have seen them coming but they don't do anything. They could have at least tried running away or something but they just sit there waiting until Darren and Wayne get there.

I can't tell exactly what's going on but it goes something like this: Darren and Wayne do their little double act of looking tough and then Macauley says something and then Wayne kicks Macauley in the stomach, pretty hard. Macauley is sitting up when he's kicked but the kick knocks him over. Then, Darren and Wayne turn to the other little kid. He fishes in his pocket and gives them something. Darren slaps him in the face but not too hard. Then the two of them walk off. It doesn't take more than a couple of minutes.

Macauley lies on the ground for a while and then he sits up. Then the two of them just carry on talking or whatever it was they were doing. I decide to go over and find out what's going on.

'Hey,' I say, walking up to them.

'Hey,' says Macauley's friend.

'What's your name?' I ask him.

'What's yours?' he replies. This sure is one suspicious school.

'I'm Mickey Sharp. I'm new around here.'

'I'm Tom Finney, this is Macauley Stone.'

Macauley's looking at me suspiciously. He doesn't look like he wants Tom to be talking to me but I'm bigger than him and his experience of bigger boys hasn't been too positive so he keeps his mouth shut. I don't think he trusts anyone.

'Me and Macauley have met. I asked his advice on a few things.'

'Oh,' says Tom. Macauley still wasn't saying anything.

'I see you know Darren and Wayne, too.'

The kid Tom looks down at the ground all of a sudden. He doesn't want to talk about Darren or Wayne. It's tough talking when nobody will look at you unless you're a teacher or something but I keep going.

'They wanted some kind of protection money out of me or something. These other guys Anthony, Nico and Giovanni were after the same thing. Is that what they were talking to you about?'

They both keep looking at the ground. I carry on.

'Look, I'm not here to cause you guys any trouble or anything. I just want to know what the situation is around here. I've been here less than a day and everybody who talks to me seems to want to get money out of me. What's going on?'

Macauley looks up and stares me straight in the eyes. He looks frightened but he looks even more angry. 'Why are you following me?'

I'm a bit taken aback by this and I kind of stutter something pathetic like I've just banged into him a few times by coincidence. It isn't so much what I say that makes me sound like I'm lying, it's the way I say it.

Macauley stands up. 'Come on,' he says to Tom, 'we're going.'

They stand up and start to walk away. I'm really pleased with myself. Another interview messed up. No chat show is ever going to give me a job. I don't usually yell after people but I'm really fed up now so I do.

'OK,' I shout. 'That's great. You just walk away. You keep paying those boys. You've got five more years in this school. How much do you think it's going to cost you or how many times you gonna get hit? All I'm trying to do is find out what's going on and maybe put a stop to it.'

Tom stops. Macauley keeps walking. Tom thinks for a second and then turns round and starts walking back towards me. Macauley stops and waits for Tom but he doesn't look back.

'You didn't get this from me, right?' is the first thing Tom says when he gets back to me. I nod.

He tells me what I need to know.

Basically it's this. There were a few bullies at the school up till three months ago but they were your normal brainless thugs and they were so dumb that even the teachers caught them and put a stop to it after a while.

Then Anthony showed up. He was different. He got them organized and got them into threatening rather than beating. This was more difficult to prove. He lets guys like Darren and Wayne believe they're doing their own thing but he runs the show. He makes sure he only picks on little kids and weedy looking new kids – it's good to know I fit into the category. He makes them pay him every week. I ask Tom why nobody told the teachers or their parents. Tom says one kid did and he ended up in hospital. The teachers suspected Anthony but he was too clever to get caught. I ask him why Macauley was getting hit. He tells me Macauley won't pay. Macauley's the only kid who they've asked who won't pay. He's upsetting their operation so they keep hitting him. I ask him why Macauley won't pay. He says you've met Macauley, haven't you? I have met him. I know what Tom's getting at; Macauley's the kind of kid who wouldn't change his mind if someone put a gun to his head. Tom says he's got to go. He walks off fast.

The bell goes.

I figure I've got as much as I'm going to get

and I decide to get out of St John's fast. I need to think.

I start walking towards the gate. The kids are going back into class. I figure that if I can get out of the school fast enough I might be able to make it back to Hanford High for the afternoon and say I've been to the dentist or something. I'm sure they'll believe me. All that Coke I drink must be rotting my teeth. But my luck's out again. As I turn out of the front gate I walk straight into the big teacher with the beard.

He grabs my arm.

'Where do you think you're going, lad?' he says.

The trouble with a uniform is that it gets you into places but it makes it really hard to get out again. I go for the innocent and stupid look.

'The dentist, sir.'

'Where's your note?'

'My note?'

'The note that says you can leave school to go to the dentist.'

'Oh, that note.'

'Yes, that note.'

'I don't know.'

'You don't know. What do you mean you don't know, lad?'

One of the things I really hate about teachers is that they really rub it in when they find a question you can't answer.

'I've lost it.'

You never know, there may be one teacher left in the world who's going to believe that one.

'Do you expect me to believe that?'

I obviously haven't found him.

'Come back into school with me, lad, and we'll see about this. Who's your form teacher?'

This is getting nasty. I need to get his hand off my arm. If he gets me back in that school I could be in big trouble.

'The note's in my bag, sir.'

'Look, lad, don't waste my time.'

'Honest, sir, I forgot.'

I try to look really dumb. If he believes I'm stupid he might just give me a chance.

He lets go of my arm.

I run.

He starts shouting. I keep running. He starts

running after me. I keep going for about a minute before looking back. When I do, he's way behind me and doubled over coughing. The good thing about adults is that they're all such physical wrecks. It's the only advantage we've got.

As soon as I can, I go down an alley and swap my uniforms. Even if he's phoned the police they'll be looking for a kid in the wrong uniform.

I check the time. It's after two. There doesn't seem much point in going back to Hanford now. I nip into a newsagent's and buy myself a Coke and a packet of crisps. I need to think.

There's a park across the road from the newsagent's so I go in there. It isn't much of a park. I wander over to the swings and sit on the only one that isn't bust. There's nobody else around, probably because of all the broken bottles lying everywhere. I take a glance at the rest of the place. The sandpit's filled with dog dirt and someone has been sick on the slide. It isn't exactly Disneyland.

I have to come up with a plan. I've done half the job, I've found out who's bullying

Macauley. The other half, of course, is to stop them. There are two ways: one is to pay Anthony off and to get him to leave Macauley alone and the other is to put him in a position where he has to stop. I don't like the first option. You can never trust guys like Anthony, once you *start* paying them, you *keep* paying them; it's no answer to anything. So I'm going to have to put him in a position where he has to stop, or where someone is going to stop *him* and his pals. This is going to be difficult.

I start thinking about the idea that you should stand up to bullies and they'll go away because deep down they're all cowards. Everybody's heard that line from someone in their time. It might be true about them all being cowards but I don't think it's the best advice in the world. It's the sort of thing that people say who aren't getting bullied. If you stand up to a bully and he's bigger than you he'll just knock you over again. Otherwise he wouldn't be a proper bully. It stands to reason. But maybe if you stand up to a bully at the right time when he's going to lose face or get caught then it might work.

I've got to get Anthony to get caught in the act. The trouble with this is that I figure that he leaves the actual bullying to his boys and just collects the money. It's no use getting Nico or Giovanni caught. If they got kicked out of school Anthony would just get some other boys. I've got to get him caught in the act of bullying and if he doesn't actually do any bullying this is going to prove tough.

I think about it some more. Nothing is coming. I get the swing moving. I have an idea. It's terrible. I get the swing going higher. I have another idea. It's even worse. I kick my legs out and get the swing really moving. I forget about Macauley Stone and Madeleine and bullying and just concentrate on getting the swing up in the air. It's getting really high now. It feels good. I haven't got a swing really moving in years. I can hear the frame creaking but I just keep going. The swing's getting so high now that the chains are going slack at the top of every arc and you feel like you're out of control. That's when the idea hits me. It's dangerous and difficult but it just might work. I fall off the swing.

I pick myself up off the ground. I'm lucky I

haven't landed on any of the broken glass. I brush off my clothes and, glancing at my watch, see that school's over for the day. I start walking home.

I get in and up to my bedroom and change out of my uniform. I stash the St John's uniform under the bed. I'm going to need it again. I keep thinking about my plan. Will it work? When it first came to me on the swing it seemed like nothing could possibly go wrong but now all I can think of are different problems. I need to get it started that evening, partly because it needs to happen quickly and partly because if I keep coming up with more problems I'll give it up altogether.

'Mickey,' my dad shouts up the stairs, 'is that you?'

'Yes,' I shout.

'Come here.'

This is the last thing I need. I want to get out and start organizing things.

'Coming.'

I go downstairs. My father's in the lounge looking out at our back garden. He doesn't turn round when I go in.

'Did you have a good day at school today?'

My heart skips a beat when he says that. If he's found out that I've bunked things are going to get very unpleasant.

'Yeah,' I say. I'm not completely lying. I have been to school today, just to the wrong one.

'Good,' he says. 'Come over here.'

I don't know what he's up to but I don't have much choice. I go over to the other side of the room.

'What do you see out of the window, Mickey?'

'Our back garden.'

'And what is the main thing in our back garden, Mickey?'

I hate it when my dad starts off on these question-and-answer sessions. There's always some answer that he wants, which is going to make you look dumb. The trouble is that he knows it and I don't.

'Grass,' I say hopefully.

'Exactly, Mickey, and what do you notice about the grass?'

I look hard at the grass and try to notice something about it.

'It's green,' I try.

My father sighs.

'Yes, it is green, Mickey, but that is not particularly noticeable about it. What about its length?'

I click what this is all about. Three weeks ago my father announced that me and my sister had to help out more around the house. I'd been volunteered to cut the grass. I don't like cutting grass so I haven't done it. I have to avoid saying that the grass is long.

'It's about normal length,' I say, trying to sound casual.

'Normal length, eh?' says my dad.

'Yeah.'

He turns round and looks at me for the first time.

'Mickey, there are jungles in South America that have shorter grass in them than that. I would be frightened to send a small person out into our garden for fear they might get lost and never find their way out again. Now get the lawnmower out and cut it.'

I could really do without gardening right now.

'Look, Dad,' I say, 'I'm busy right now. I'll

do it in a couple of days.'

'You'll do it now.'

'Dad.'

'Now.'

There's nothing for it. I go and get the lawn-mower out. I hate my dad being unemployed, it just gives him more time to think of methods to torment me.

I cut the grass as fast as I can. I'm just putting the mower away when my dad appears and offers the view that he thinks it's a novel idea to leave the grass with about fifteen different lengths but he's a bit old fashioned and would like it all the same. So I cut it again.

By the time I've got every blade of grass to be two centimetres high it's time for tea. At this rate I'm never going to get my plan going.

The conversation at the table is the normal bickering about money. I'm not paying much attention as it's always the same, there isn't enough for whatever we want. Yelling at each other isn't going to make us richer, is it? Anyway, I'm trying to eat as quickly as possible so I can get away. My dad with an unerring eye for spotting things to criticize notices this.

'Mickey,' he says, looking at me with obvious distaste, 'someone said to me that you weren't fit to eat with pigs but I defended you. I said you were.'

My dad has said this to me about a thousand times and he still thinks it's funny.

'Thanks, Dad,' I say, 'it's nice to know you can rely on your parents for support.'

My father ignores me and turns to my mother.

'Did we not teach him how to eat like a civilized human being? He uses his fork like a shovel and his mouth like a gigantic bin.'

My mother doesn't say anything.

I finish my plate and stand up to leave.

'Mickey,' says my mother, 'it's polite to wait till everybody else has finished before leaving the table.'

'Like it's polite to tell people they eat like pigs?' I say. I'm getting angry.

'I'm your father. It's my job,' says my dad, looking smug now he knew he'd got to me.

'Yeah, it's the one job nobody can sack you from, isn't it?'

There was a bit of a silence after I say that. Nobody's supposed to mention the fact that my dad got sacked. I kind of know I've gone too far but I was happily keeping my head down until he started picking on me.

'Just go, Mickey,' says my mother.

So I go.

I'm not feeling too good as I walk over to where Tom Finney lives. He's the kid who walked home with Macauley the evening I followed him so I know where he lives. I need his help. Macauley isn't ever going to trust me because I made such a fool of myself trying to talk to him last week but Tom just might. I'm not really bothered though. I don't really care about Macauley or any of the other stuff at the moment but I have to get out of the house and Tom Finney's is as good a place to go as any. I'm feeling like giving everything up and running away somewhere but there isn't anywhere to go. I'm stuck.

I knock on the door of Tom's house when I get there. His mother opens the door.

I ask her if Tom's in. She looks me up and

down and obviously doesn't like what she sees. Story of my life.

'I'll see,' she says.

I wait around for a couple of minutes and Tom comes to the door. I can hear his mother in the background saying, 'Just five minutes, Tom. You've got homework, remember.' He doesn't look particularly happy to see me.

'How did you find out where I live?' he says.

'Lucky guess,' I tell him.

'Very funny.'

'Listen,' I say, 'I need your help.'

'Well, you can't have it. Goodbye.' He's cocky for an eleven-year-old even taking into account the fact that he's standing on his own doorstep. He makes like he's going to shut the door in my face. I put my foot in the way.

'It'll get Anthony and Darren and Wayne off your back for good.'

He decides not to shut the door. He looks tempted.

'Give me a couple of minutes,' I say to him, trying to sound like I believe in myself. 'If you don't like it you just close the door and I disappear. What harm can it do?'

Never trust anyone who talks to you like that even if it's me, they are trying to sell you something you don't want. This kid isn't as clever as he thinks because he stays and listens. Five minutes later I have him hooked.

I walk home feeling more cheerful. If being a detective doesn't work out, at least I can be a double glazing salesman. Then I think that if this kind of thought is cheering me up, I really am in trouble.

CHAPTER SIX

The next day I decide I'm going to be the sort of kid that makes you want to vomit. My plan is only going to work if I don't get into any trouble all day, and then I'll be free to do what I need to do tomorrow.

I get up early, I help tidy up the house without being told, I go to school (the right school this time) before the bell. I remember my note to give to Mr Newman explaining my absence (all right, it was faked but nobody's perfect). I answer questions in my first two lessons and I even get some of them right.

By the time that the bell goes at breaktime, I'm already tired of being Superpupil but I'm determined that I'm going to keep it up. I wander out onto the playground, sit down, pull a Coke out of my bag and start thinking again about whether my plan is going to work. One problem is . . .

'Hello, Mickey.'

I look up. Standing over me is Katie Pierce.

'Hi,' I say, trying to make 'hi' sound as much like 'go away' as possible.

She sits down next to me. This is odd. We're in the same class but I don't think we've ever talked to each other much. That's the way I want our relationship to stay.

'Look,' I say, 'I don't want to be rude but I'm a bit busy at the moment.'

'I don't see you doing anything,' she says.

'I'm thinking,' I say.

She starts laughing when I say that.

'Be very careful about trying new things, Mickey,' she says, smiling at me.

I look away. I don't want to get involved in an argument with her. This is supposed to be the day when I do nothing wrong and believe me if you get into an argument with Katie Pierce, you've no idea how it's going to end up.

'What are you thinking about?' she asks sweetly. Too sweetly.

'Stuff,' I say.

I have no idea why Katie Pierce is talking to me but one rule worth sticking to is never tell her anything. I've seen far too many people who've told Katie Pierce their secrets and who've found out that the whole class knows about them the next day.

'I'm glad to see you're better.'

'What?' I say, a bit quicker than I should have.

'Well, I noticed that you weren't in the last lesson on Thursday or Friday and then you were off yesterday.'

'I still don't feel brilliant,' I say. 'That's why I'm not really in the mood to talk.'

'I thought you said you were thinking.' Suddenly all the concern disappears out of her voice.

'I was thinking about whether I was still ill.'

'Oh,' she says.

There is a bit of a pause. I start thinking about getting away from her.

'It's funny how your illness came on in the last lesson two days running, isn't it?' she says.

I don't say anything.

'And then you were off on Monday. Now, it's a strange thing but a friend of mine who goes to St John's is certain he saw you there yesterday, in a St John's uniform.'

I freeze.

'Now, I know you're not the cleverest boy in our class, Mickey, but I'm sure that even you can remember which school we go to.'

'He must have made a mistake,' I say, keeping my eyes staring straight down at the grass at my feet.

'Well, whatever. The thing is, Mickey, that what with you disappearing before the end of school two days running last week and then hearing that you'd gone into a different school yesterday, well, it puts me in a very difficult position, doesn't it?'

'Why?' I say. 'It's none of your business.'

'Oh, but it is my business, Mickey. You see, as your classmate and as a good pupil of Hanford High, I feel that it is my duty to tell Mr Newman about what's been going on.'

A quick vision of how much trouble I would be in if Newman found out about everything I'd been doing in the past few days flicks across my mind. I start sweating.

'What do you want, Katie?' I say. All that 'good pupil of Hanford High' stuff was garbage. This is good old-fashioned blackmail and I'm going to have to pay whatever she asks.

'To help you, Mickey, that's all.'

'By grassing me up.'

'Sometimes you have to be cruel to be kind.'

This is getting annoying.

'Look, Katie,' I say. 'You know and I know that you want something. Just tell me what it is.'

'I don't know what you're talking about. I don't want anything.'

I don't say anything.

'Oh, except for one thing,' she says.

Now we were getting to it.

'What?' I say.

'Ask me out.'

'What?'

I'm so shocked that I look straight at her.

'Ask me out,' she repeats, staring right back at me.

When I said that I was going to have to pay whatever she asked I didn't realize that the price was going to be this high. Some guys would take one look at Katie Pierce and think I was mad not to ask her out. She's really good-looking and everything. Some guys will tell you that's all they ever look for when they decide who they should ask out. But Katie Pierce is the sort of girl who cures you of that attitude when you've known her for a while. I've seen the guys she goes out with. She tells them what to do all the time and laughs at them in front of her friends and makes them look dumb. And they put up with it. I reckon most of them are too frightened to finish with her.

But if I don't ask her out she'll tell Newman. One thing about Katie is that she carries out her threats. She's not bluffing. And apart from all the trouble that I'd get into there's no chance I'd be able to carry out my plan tomorrow and that would mean that none of the bullying would stop at St John's and it would ruin my chances with Madeleine.

'Look, Katie,' I say trying to sound honest, 'I mean I like you and everything. I'm just not sure that we'd be able to go out together. I haven't got much money and I wouldn't be able to take you out anywhere . . .'

She starts laughing.

'What are you laughing for?' I say.

'Oh, Mickey, you're funny,' she says. 'I told

you to ask me out. I didn't say that I was going to say yes.'

'But why do you want me to ask you out if you're not going to say yes?' I say.

And so she tells me.

I knew she was bad but I didn't think she was this bad. I didn't think anyone was this bad. And she's got me right in the palm of her hand.

I have never eaten a plate of chips slower than I do this lunchtime. I put salt, vinegar and tomato sauce on. I eat them one by one, chewing each one about a thousand times before I swallow it. And with the taste of the chips that they serve in our school canteen that takes some effort.

And all the time I'm trying to put off what I have to do but I know I can't. It's like this. Katie will tell Newman on me unless I ask her out and let her say no. But I don't just have to ask her out. That would be too easy. I have to ask her out in front of all her friends. Imagine that. Having to ask someone out in front of all their friends and be rejected. I've been imagining little else since she told me.

What kind of sick person comes up with an idea like that? Katie Pierce, that's who. And do you know why she wants me to do this? Because Julie Reece has been asked out twice in the last couple of weeks. Julie Reece is Katie's best friend so you'd think she'd be pleased for her. No way. Katie has always been asked out more than Julie and as far as she's concerned, that's the way things are going to stay. So, I have to ask her out in front of all her friends so nobody can say that she's making it up. All I can say is that some girls are very frightening.

But, however slow you chew them, in the end chips go and when these chips are gone I have to put my plate onto the pile, walk out of the dining room and head towards the far end of the playground.

I can see them all the whole time I'm walking there. Katie Pierce, Julie Reece, Susan Ashe, Louise Petch and Anne Bower. As I get nearer I see that they are smoking a cigarette and passing it round between them. I've never understood that. Ms Hardy and Ms Walter are always telling our class that girls are more mature than boys, they're more sensible. If that's right, how come it's always the girls you see smoking cigarettes? I mean cigarettes cost you loads of money, give you cancer and make you smell bad. If that's mature, I'm glad I'm not.

I walk up towards them.

'Hello, Mickey,' says Susan Ashe. 'You want a drag of my fag?'

I shake my head.

'It would make him cough,' says Anne Bower.

They all laugh.

'Take a chance, Mickey,' says Louise Petch.

'I'm OK,' I say.

'What do you want then?' says Julie Reece.

'I want to talk to Katie,' I say.

Katie has been looking the other way up to now. She probably thinks that's acting natural but it's not. She'd have been the first to have a go at me normally. She turns round when she hears me say her name trying to act all surprised. She's a lousy actress but none of her friends seem to notice.

'What do you want, Mickey?' she asks.

'I wanted to ask you something,' I say.

Things are going to get very hard from now on.

'Ask away,' she says.

I look down at the floor and try to imagine I'm talking to Madeleine.

'I was wondering if maybe you wanted to go to a movie or something this weekend.'

A big 'Oooh' goes up from all the girls.

'A movie?' says Katie. She isn't going to let me off easy.

'Yeah. Or do something else if you want,' I say.

'Like what?'

This girl doesn't just want to humiliate you. She likes to torture you first.

'I don't know. Whatever.'

I put a bit of snap into my voice to let Katie know I think she's pushing it a bit.

'Just me and you?'

There's no stopping her. She's going to get every ounce of humiliation out of me that she can.

'Yeah,' I say though I'm tempted to tell her she can bring her granny if she wants.

'Like a date?'

'Yeah. A date.'

'Well, I don't know what I'm doing this weekend. Why me? There are so many girls you could go for in this school.'

The next bit is the worst of all. She'd written it down for me and said I had to memorize it. I stare really hard at a stone which is lying on the playground and clench my fist so hard that I can feel the nails biting into the skin.

'I just fancy you,' I begin. 'I've fancied you ever since we started at school and I never had the courage to ask you out before but I've got to take that chance now or some other guy might get you because I know so many of them really like you.'

I say the words like a robot. I mean, even to me, they don't make any sense. Think about it. If I've fancied Katie for three years and never had the courage to ask her out, why would I suddenly be doing it in front of four other people. But the other girls don't seem to notice. Still, they all spend their time reading those teen magazines with photo love stories. They probably think people talk like that in real life.

'Well,' says Katie, 'that's really nice,

Mickey. I never had any idea that you felt like that about me or that so many other boys did.'

She sure is making certain that her friends get the message that she's the most attractive girl on the block.

'I was totally unprepared for you fancying me, Mickey,' she carries on, 'but because you've had the courage to come up and ask me out when all those other boys who want to haven't got the guts, then, what the hell, I'll go out with you.'

I nearly die on the spot. This is worse, much worse than I could ever have imagined. My eyes shoot themselves up from the ground and stare at her in shock.

'What?' I say dumbly. 'You will?'

Katie takes a drag from the fag she has in her hand. All the other girls are looking at her too. I don't think they'd expected her to say yes either. She has the smoke in her mouth for what seems like an age and then blows it out slowly.

'What a sucker,' she says. 'Don't you know I never go out with anyone under sixteen?'

She drops her fag on to the ground and stubs it out with her toe.

All her friends start laughing.

Katie walks past me, shaking her head, and the others follow her. I can hear them laughing all the way back to the school.

Our Physics teacher reckons that the thing that travels fastest in the world is light. He's wrong. The thing that travels fastest in the world is the news that you've just asked someone out in your class and they've said no. By the time the first lesson starts after lunch, everybody knows.

As soon as I walk into the room it starts,

'Mickey got turned down.'

'Has she broken your heart, Mickey?'

'Don't cry, Mickey.'

The morons at the back are having the time of their lives.

'Katie, you're wonderful.'

'Katie, you're fantastic.'

'Katie, I think I love you.'

Situations like these are the worst in the world. If you don't say anything back they keep getting at you until you do. If you do say anything they think they've got to you and they get even worse. The best thing to do would be to disappear off the face of the earth for a month or two until everyone has forgotten about it. Unfortunately, I can't do this today as I'm supposed to be being Mr Perfect and making sure I don't do anything wrong.

I give them this sarcastic smile as if to say, 'Don't you think you're being a bit pathetic?' and go and sit down. They laugh even more. Trying to make morons at the back ashamed of themselves is a bit like trying to explain to a group of piranha fish that eating people just isn't very nice.

I take a look at Katie. I know it's stupid but I just can't help it. The girls who are sitting near her give her a nudge and she looks up at me. She gives me these big brown eyes, like she's saying, 'I'm sorry I broke your heart but it just wasn't meant to be.' She could win an Oscar. All the girls sitting round her look at me like I'm a baby rabbit and go, 'Aaah.'

This is even worse than having the morons at the back laughing at me.

Then, Umair comes up to me and says, 'You really asked Katie out?'

He looks confused. I can't really blame him. We had a conversation once about the person in our class we would least like to be stuck on a desert island with. I went for Katie Pierce.

I want to tell him the truth. It's bad enough when it's the morons at the back who don't know what's going on but when it's someone who used to be your friend it's even worse. But I can't. It's part of my deal with Katie that I don't tell anybody and I can't break it when she's watching.

'Yeah,' I shrug.

He stares at me for a second like he's going to say something else but then he seems to decide not to. He just nods and walks back to his place.

'Good afternoon, everybody.'

It's Miss Hurley. Never have I been happier to see a teacher.

'Can we all settle down and get our coats off and our bags off the desk and get ready to do some good work? Julie, can you give out the poetry books, please?'

Julie gets up and starts handing out the books. That's the good thing about Miss Hurley; she knows how to handle our class. If it had been some of the other teachers everybody would have ignored her when she said,

'Settle down,' and she would have had to start yelling before anyone did anything. And Julie would have moaned about giving out the books and said it was someone else's turn and there would have been a big argument. With Miss Hurley you just do what she says without thinking about it. I don't know why you do it for her and not for some of the others. I guess some teachers have it and some teachers don't.

'Right,' says Miss Hurley, 'today we will be looking at some love poetry.'

I feel sick. Love is the one subject I would rather avoid at the moment.

'Now, turn to page 124 and let us see what William Shakespeare has to say about love.'

There is a bit of a groan when the class hears it's Shakespeare. According to Miss Hurley, he's the greatest writer ever. Well, that might be true but he doesn't always make sense.

'I don't want to hear any moans,' says Miss Hurley. 'If you only gave him a chance you would find that Shakespeare more than repays your efforts. Now, who is going to read?'

The morons at the back take their chance.

'Mickey.'

'Mickey's good at reading.'

'Mickey will put some feeling into it.'

Miss Hurley looks at me.

'I prefer volunteers to conscripts, as we know,' she says, 'but Mickey, you haven't read for a while.'

She looks over at me. I don't normally believe in asking teachers for favours but I can't face reading a love poem with the whole class knowing what's going on. I give her a little shake of my head.

'No,' she says. The way she says it I know she's caught on that something was happening. 'I think, after all, we should have one of those who bravely tried to volunteer someone else. Robert Foster, I'm sure that you will give us a wonderful reading of the poem.'

Foster's one of the morons at the back. The other two start laughing at him. That's the thing about the morons. They don't even stick together.

Anyway, Foster reads this poem like it's the telephone directory and then Miss Hurley reads it again. She reads it better than Foster but I still don't really understand it.

Then, she tells us to write our own love poem. I can't say I really feel like it. I reckon it's stupid telling people just to write a love poem. I bet nobody told Shakespeare to do it. I reckon he probably only wrote them when he was in the mood. But you can't say that to Miss Hurley. 'When you can write as well as Shakespeare, I'll treat you like Shakespeare,' she says.

Anyway, about five minutes from the end of the lesson, Miss Hurley says, 'Right. Stop writing now. Would anybody like to read their poem to the class?'

This is the time when everyone avoids catching Miss Hurley's eye. There is nothing worse than reading your poem to the class. Especially if it's a love poem. If it was about football, it wouldn't be as bad.

'Katie's poem's really good,' says Julie.

'Will you read it to us, Katie?' says Miss Hurley.

Katie is up in front of the class real fast. I get a hollow feeling in my stomach.

'My poem,' says Katie, 'is called *All the Boys like You*. It's based on my own personal experience.'

'Get on with it, Katie,' says Miss Hurley.

I don't really know whether I believe in God or not but it's at times like these that you say a prayer anyway.

Katie coughs, '"All The Boys Like You" by Katie Pierce:

He came up to me at lunchtime
When I was having a fag.
He said, "Can I talk to you?"
And put down his bag.

He said, "Katie, all the boys like you
But I like you the best.
I like you better
Than all the rest."

"Will you go out with me?"
He said to me.
"We could go out lots of places
Like a movie."

"Although you really fancy me,"
I said to him
"I can't go out with you.
It would be a sin."

I thought that he would cry
So I said, "Be brave,
I won't go out with anyone
Who doesn't even shave."

The End.'

Everybody is killing themselves with laughter by the time she finishes. Miss Hurley says she thought it was rather shallow. Katie looks really pleased with herself. The bell goes. I get out of that classroom and out of that school fast. Whatever it takes, I will get Katie Pierce back for that poem. Whatever it takes.

After the day I've had the last thing I feel like doing is seeing anyone. What I really want to do is to go back home, get a Coke, sit down in my shed with a packet of crisps and work out some horrible revenge on Katie Pierce. But I don't have that option. All the things I've done for her today have been designed to give me a shot at sorting this case out. I can't throw it all away now.

I get on my bike and head for the park where I've arranged to meet Tom Finney. I stop off on the way and change into my St

John's uniform. I don't want them to know I don't go to their school or they might stop trusting me. They're already there when I get there. Eight little eleven-year-olds (including Tom and Macauley). I'd asked Tom for ten but he said only six would come. Macauley is there but he's standing a little bit apart from the group. I look at them and believe in my plan even less.

I try not to let my feelings show. Nobody's going to believe in you if you don't look like you believe in yourself. I get ready for my big speech.

'OK,' I start, 'we're here because we are fed up being kicked around and we want to do something about it, right?'

I pause for them to agree but it is a mistake because they don't. Still, they don't say no either. I carry on.

'We all know how bullies work. They get you on your own in places where they can't be seen and where they're bigger than you and there are more of them.'

That last sentence comes out wrong but I think they get the message.

'The only way to stop them is to stand up to

them and to stand up to them in numbers and at the right time. You together are the numbers and I'm going to make sure it's the right time.'

I figure I could make a politician one day. I don't have the faintest idea what I'm saying but they are beginning to nod a bit.

'And sometimes we've got to remember that when we're fighting against someone like Anthony we can't always be too honest. We've got to be prepared to tell the odd lie now and again.'

I'm getting a bit carried away with my speech but Tom has heard it all before and he isn't.

'Tell them about the plan,' he says.

I take his advice.

'The idea is this,' I say. 'Tom is going to go and see Anthony and tell him Macauley is going to pay but he wants to pay him and not Wayne and Darren. Anthony will bring along Nico and Giovanni because from what I hear he never goes anywhere without them. Then Tom's going to see Wayne and Darren and tell them that Macauley decided he's sick of being kicked about and he's going to pay up to them, not to Anthony and his boys. Tom's going to tell them all Macauley will meet them behind the sports hall during break. We've got to get all five of them in the same place at the same time if we're going to make sure that we stop all of them bullying at once. When they get there they'll probably be a bit confused because Anthony and his boys won't expect Darren and Wayne to be there and Darren and Wayne won't expect Anthony and his boys to be there. This is where you lot come in. You're going to be behind the sports hall too. This is where the fun starts.'

An extra meeting with the bullies doesn't look like it is going to appeal to my audience so I get on with the second half of my plan. They aren't completely convinced when I've finished which doesn't surprise me because neither am I. I go back to my politician bit. 'Look,' I say, 'if you don't do this you're quitting. You're just rolling over and dying and you'll be doing it for the rest of your life because the world is filled with Darrens and Waynes and Anthonys. They're only hard because you let them be hard. If you stop giving in to them then they're nothing. Now, come on.'

I don't know where these speeches are coming from. My dad tells me that all I do is grunt most of the time and that he reckons it's a miracle when I actually manage to string two words together. He's exaggerating but he's got a point. I'm not big on talking.

Still, looking at my audience I seem to be having some kind of effect. They seem to be believing what I am saying. What is even stranger is the fact that I'm beginning to believe it too.

'I'm in,' says Tom. 'How about the rest of you?'

Slowly, one by one, they start nodding until Macauley is the only one left who won't say he'll do it. This is annoying. He's the only one I really need. I look at the other little kids and feel angry. What right does he have to stay out of this and leave this lot to get bullied again?

'All right,' I say. 'We'll have to leave it. We need Macauley and he won't help us out. Thanks a lot, kid. See you around.'

I turn round and start to walk off.

'Hey,' shouts a voice.

I turn round. It's Macauley.

'I'm in,' he says.

Thank God for that. I would have felt a right moron just walking off.

'Right,' I say, 'see you all tomorrow.'

It's like I'm their dad or something. As soon as I say go, they walk off. I watch them go, feeling a little bit proud and a big bit worried. They are about to disappear when I remember something.

'Tom,' I yell. 'What's the name of the big teacher with the beard?'

'Braithwaite,' he yells back.

If I'd forgotten to find that out, tomorrow could have turned into a blood bath.

I get back home about half an hour later and head down to the shed. I don't fancy meeting any of my family again for a while. I've picked up a Coke and a packet of crisps on my way back. I'm going to eat them, nice and slow.

I open the door and switch on the light. There's a note on the floor. I pick it up and read it.

Mickey, it says (I'm obviously not worth a *Dear Mickey*), *Are you getting anywhere with this case or are you just sitting about doing nothing? I want some results. I will be back tomorrow. Be here. Madeleine.*

She is one demanding girl.

Still, if it all works out tomorrow she'll have more results than she expects, and maybe I'll see some results too.

CHAPTER SEVEN

I don't sleep too well that night and I wake up feeling like my brain has stayed asleep. I jam my head under the shower for about twenty minutes and feel a bit more lively. I stick on my Hanford High Uniform, shove my St John's uniform into my bag and head downstairs for breakfast. My mother's down there looking like she does in the morning, which is old. She never sleeps well. It's something to do with stress. I'm beginning to understand what people mean when they talk about stress. The pressure's getting to me.

'Mickey,' my mother says.

'Yeah.'

'Can you be a bit nicer to your father? He's not feeling very well at the moment.'

'OK,' I say, and start pouring out the corn flakes.

'Don't just say "OK" like that to shut me up. I want you to mean it.'

I can really do without this right now.

'Well, he's not always that nice to me.'

'He's going through a bad time at the moment.'

'He's always going through a bad time.'

'You're *so* selfish, Mickey.'

She stands up and walks out of the room.

A family argument. Just what I need to start my day.

I get out of the house fast and head to the park where I get changed into my St John's uniform. I've about an hour and a half to kill before the action starts. I hope Tom made sure that he found Anthony and Darren and gave them the message about being behind the sports hall at break, or else the whole thing will fall apart. I hope Macauley keeps out of sight until break so they can't get him beforehand, and I hope that none of the other kids woke up this morning and decided that standing up to the bullies was a bad idea after all.

The park is looking its usual disgusting self. I go over to my swing but it's proved too tempting a target to someone and they've smashed the seat in two last night. Well, it's been asking for it. It was the only thing that wasn't broken in the whole place.

I wander over to the pond. It has two supermarket trolleys sticking out of it and the water's brown and stinks like a school toilet. I look into it but I can't see any fish.

There's a bench nearby which is only smashed up at one end so I go and sit on it and wait. I thought that maybe I'd get better at the waiting with practice. I figured that I might be able to sort of switch myself off and time would whizz by. It isn't turning out that way. Time is going slower than I ever thought it could. I keep telling myself not to look at my watch because every time I do it seems to have gone forward by a tiny amount. I reckon that if I stay in this park long enough, time will start going backwards.

But it doesn't. Slowly it advances and eventually it reaches five minutes to go before the bell for break. I walk down to St John's and wait as near as I can to the gate without letting anyone from the school see me.

The bell goes.

Thirty seconds later I walk into the school just as the kids are beginning to spill out onto the playground. Tom and Macauley and five of the other little kids I'd talked to yesterday are out fast and heading over to the sports hall. There should have been another kid. Maybe one of them has become mysteriously ill over night. Yellow fever, no doubt. Still, seven will be enough.

Tom looks round to where I'd told him I'd be and gives me the thumbs up sign. This means that he's got the message to Darren and Wayne and to Anthony and his boys. All we have to do now is hope they all show up.

Five minutes go by with nothing happening. Well, nothing that I'm waiting for anyway. There's your normal break time stuff – kids kicking a ball about, kids arguing, kids stuffing their faces full of chocolate and kids sneaking off for a fag. A couple of teachers appear at one point, which I'm a bit concerned about, but they don't stray far from the door. They chat for a bit, drink their coffee and go back inside.

At last, I see Anthony and his boys and they are heading to the right place. Where are Darren and Wayne? They're so dumb that when you give them the clearest directions in the world they get it wrong. I want them all there but I can't rely on Macauley and Tom being able to stall Anthony and his boys for too long.

Anthony and his boys go round the corner. This is my signal to go but Darren and Wayne are nowhere to be seen. I've said to the little kids that they only need to occupy the bullies for four minutes. By which time the cavalry will arrive.

Finally, I spot Darren and Wayne. But it isn't good news. They are walking away from the sports hall. They've forgotten about the meeting. I close my eyes for five seconds and pray they'll turn round. I open them again. They're still walking away from the sports hall.

I look at my watch. Things are taking too long. The whole plan is going to fall apart.

There's nothing for it, I'm going to have to get them there. I start to run towards them.

'Hey,' I yell as I get near them. I'm not going to go too near.

'What?' says Darren

'Anthony's nicking your clients,' I say.

'Oh. . .' says Darren.

'Yeah,' says Wayne.

'Behind the sports hall. Macauley's giving him money. Beat me up if it's not true,' I say and run off towards the school.

I glance back just before I enter the building. Darren and Wayne are heading towards the sports hall.

I get into the school and walk as fast as I can without attracting attention towards the staff room. Tom's told me exactly where it is. I get there fast. There're a few kids hanging around outside. I shove my way through them and knock hard on the door.

A teacher opens it pretty quickly.

'I need to see Mr Braithwaite,' I say.

'You're not supposed to disturb teachers during their break,' the teacher says.

'He told me to come here,' I say. 'He told me I'd be in trouble if I didn't.'

The teacher looks at me and then turns round.

'Frank,' he shouts, 'a kid for you.'

I hear something get shouted back but I don't hear what it is. The teacher turns back.

'He'll be here in a minute,' he says and shuts the door.

This is not good. I'm already behind schedule. Over behind the sports hall Macauley and Tom are telling Anthony that they and all the other kids want to reduce the payments they are making him. That's why they are all there. If he doesn't agree they'll stop paying him. I've told them they have to argue with him until I get there but they aren't going to be able to keep arguing for ever.

I stare at the closed door. Come on, come on, I say to myself.

The door opens and Braithwaite stands there. I've been worrying in case he doesn't recognize me but he recognizes me all right. His face goes very red.

'You, boy,' he yells. 'I've been searching the school for you for two days. You are in so much trouble.'

I look at him straight in the face.

'You're fat and you're ugly,' I say and I turn and run.

I'm not sure that the last insult was strictly necessary but I need to make sure he comes after me.

He comes after me all right. He gives this huge bellow first but when I keep moving he starts running. I head off down the corridor. I try not to run too fast because I don't want him to give up or have a heart attack or something. This is tougher than I imagined because my legs are ignoring my brain. They're scared and they're trying to run as fast as they can. He's still coming, though. I can hear him wheezing.

I round the corner of the corridor and head in the direction of the playground. There's a teacher at the far end. He's looking the other way. Braithwaite must have come round the corner because I hear him yell out, 'Ron, stop that kid, will you?' The teacher at the far end turns round. I run towards him, pretend I'm going one way and then run the other. His hand touches my jumper as I go by. But I'm out.

I head straight for the sports hall. I have two teachers after me now. I keep running thinking that I'm going to fall over at any minute. I check behind me. They are about ten metres behind me. Not quite enough. I dig deep and put on a final sprint as I get to the sports hall. As soon as they see me the kids go into action.

What I see when I go round the corner is five little kids jumping on five big kids, whilst two other little kids fall on the ground and start rolling round in what looks like a lot of pain. Now, what would you do if you were a big sixteen-year-old bully and a little eleven-year-old attacked you? You'd throw him on to the floor and being a bully you might even kick him a couple of times as well. Which is exactly what Braithwaite and Ron see when they come round the corner five seconds later. Five sixteen-year-olds laying into five eleven-year-olds with two other eleven-year-olds lying on the ground in agony having already been beaten up.

Discovering that they've just run into World War Three the teachers forget about me and launch into splitting up the fights. Braithwaite pulls Anthony off his eleven-year-old not re-alizing that the eleven-year-old had started it all and slams him hard into the sports hall wall. I start to like Braithwaite a bit after all. The bullies look completely confused. They can't understand what's happening to them.

Ron has Darren by the hair and Wayne by the arm. Everybody is yelling like crazy. It's fantastic to watch.

Lots of other kids are heading over to the scene. Kids have some kind of ESP when it comes to trouble. They always know when something worth watching is going on. The trouble is they make it so obvious they attract teachers too. Already another couple are running over. I want to stay and watch but I know that Braithwaite will remember me soon. I need to get out of St John's before I get caught because I'll have to come up with the best lie ever to explain away this one.

I take one last look. Braithwaite has Anthony by the collar and is yelling at him about being a thug and a bully. Anthony is shouting that the little kid attacked him. Braithwaite shakes Anthony like he is a doll and screams, 'Don't lie to me, boy. You're pathetic.' The little kids who Anthony claims have attacked him are all lying on the floor looking like they only have moments to live. I reckon they could all be actors when they grow up. They even look like they've been beaten up to me and I know they haven't. I turn around and head for the gate. Case closed.

Of course it never works out just how you imagine it will. I get back to Hanford High feeling like a genius and sneak into Maths and tell the teacher I've been to the dentist. He tells me that he has a message that if I showed up I had to go to the deputy head's office. I should have sensed something was wrong but I was thinking about the morning at St John's. So, I knock at the door and go in. Who's there? The deputy head, Mr Newman and my dad. Anthony isn't the only one who is going to get caught today.

It's my own fault for not noticing that Mr Newman was getting better as a teacher. He's noticed my attendance and lateness and thought he'd seen me leaving school early last week. He's done some checking. He's rung my dad and here they all are and they want some answers. Teachers – they may be slow but they catch up with you in the end.

I won't bore you with all the lies I have to tell. I wouldn't mind telling them the truth for once but do you think they'd believe that I've spent the last few days saving a whole group of eleven-year-olds from being bullied in another school? I don't think so. But if the lies are boring, the lectures are even worse. I have one from the deputy, two from Newman and so many from my dad that I lose count. In the end I just switch off and say, 'Yes,' or, 'I'm sorry,' whenever there's a pause in the telling off. It seems to do the trick.

The school punishes me with detentions for a week, extra work and by making me go and see the school counsellor once a week. My dad punishes me by making me do every job in the house he can think of and then, when he runs out of them, he sends me round to my gran's to do all her jobs too. She's never been happier. She follows me round telling me how ungrateful I am.

I can't even keep my appointment with Madeleine. I leave a note telling her that I'll meet her same time same place next week and that Macauley won't be getting any more bruises at school. Thinking about Madeleine is about the only thing that keeps me sane.

CHAPTER EIGHT

One week later the heat has cooled off a bit and I'm no longer Public Enemy Number One. I am sitting in my chair in the shed waiting for Madeleine.

I've managed to sort one little thing out though. Getting caught means that I no longer have to worry about Katie grassing me up. They can't punish you more than once for the same offence can they?

So, I use my father's camera one day. It's got a zoom lens which means you can take close-up photos of people without them noticing. The photos they get of celebrities in the papers are all done with a zoom lens. My dad's isn't that good but it is enough to catch Katie Pierce smoking on the far side of the school playground. I get the photos developed that night and pick them up the next day. That morning, I take the register back after registration. I nip into the toilets and have a quick glance under Katie's name. There is her address. Then, I post the photos to her mum. I wouldn't normally involve parents in stuff like this. It isn't really too fair but I figure if Katie could break the rules then I can too.

The next morning, in registration, the girls are talking about this party. It's at this sixteen-year-old lad's house so they're all going crazy about it. Girls always seem to think older lads are better. They always say sixteen-year-olds are more mature. I don't understand that. Most sixteen-year-old lads spend half their time at parties drinking loads of cheap cider and the other half puking it up. They think that's cool? Still, you'll never convince the girls. Once they've decided that some guy is mature, they'll go on believing it even if they find out he still wears a nappy.

Katie isn't talking much, when they are going on about this party, which is unusual – normally she talks twice as much as everybody else and twice as loud. Then, she mutters something about not being able to go because she's been grounded for two months after her mother found out that she smokes. She sees me listening in when she says this. 'Mind your own business,' she says.

'Sorry,' I say, 'but you know I can't take my eyes off you. But maybe if I had a picture of you, I could look at that instead. Have you got any photos that have been taken lately?'

There is a beautiful moment when her mouth opens in surprise. People like Katie think they can treat you like dirt all the time and then they're shocked when you give them a taste of their own medicine.

Mind you, I'm not kidding myself. If you mess with Katie Pierce, she'll come back after you. But just for now, I'm in the driving seat and it feels good.

I'm recreating this magic moment when there's a knock on the door and in comes Madeleine. She looks incredible. Any doubts I've had that it's going to be worth it disappear out of my mind.

She doesn't sit down but leans against the far corner of the shed looking at me.

'So, Mickey,' she says in that deep smooth voice she has, 'you solved the case.'

I nod. I checked it out with Tom during the week. Anthony and his boys were all suspended and are going to be expelled in two weeks. I hope they don't end up in Hanford High. We've got too many headcases already. The little kids have all told about the protection racket, after hearing that no teacher was going to listen to Anthony telling them he'd been set up.

Madeleine begins to walk slowly round the shed. My eyes follow her like they are on a lead. She moves lazily round to my side of the desk. She stares at me. I stare back. My eyes aren't going anywhere else.

'Maybe I underestimated your abilities,' she says.

I shrug.

'Well, I'd like to thank you,' she says staring at me, 'but how? What can a girl like me give a boy like you?'

I don't say anything. She reaches into her pocket and pulls out a packet.

'Gum?' she says, offering me a stick.

This isn't the kind of reward I have in mind. I shake my head.

She unwraps a stick and puts it into her mouth. She starts chewing, staring at me all the time. I regret not taking the gum. My throat feels dry.

'Maybe I can think of something,' she says.

She leans forward so her face is right in front of mine. I can't move. My eyes stare into hers. Her face moves towards mine. I close my eyes.

Suddenly she isn't there. I open my eyes. She's already by the door looking at me with a wicked smile on her face.

'You said three pounds a day, didn't you? I threw in a little extra as a tip. I'll see you round, Mickey.'

And then she's gone.

I look down into my lap to see two ten pound notes lying there. I pick them up and look at the Queen's face staring out at me. Her face is old and she has a double chin. She looks amused. I scrumple her up and put her in my pocket.

I open a drawer and pull out a bottle of

Coke. I give the top a vicious twist and the bubbles fizz up angrily. I take a long swig. It's been a hell of a week and I need to calm down.

THE END

ABOUT THE AUTHOR

Dominic Barker was born in Southport in 1966. At school, Dominic was given the prestigious task of looking after the locusts in the Biology lab. Soon, however, the glamour of this job faded and he lapsed into a sullen adolescence for the next decade. He eventually emerged from the University of Birmingham with a degree in English without having once broken into a smile.

After graduating, Dominic worked as a stand-up comedian. However, the search for something slightly more secure (though equally open to heckling), led him to qualify as a teacher. He taught in London for a number of years, emerging with greying hair, a damaged psyche and the desire to be a writer.

Dominic's inside knowledge of contemporary classroom life and his witty observations of the teenage world give a unique edge to *Sharp Stuff*, his first novel. Great reviews and a shortlisting for the Branford Boase Award for first novels for children greeted its publication in 1999. *Sharp Shot*, his second book, followed two years later to further acclaim.

Dominic is currently living in Dorset, where he continues to teach and write.

SHARP SHOT
Dominic Barker

It's not like in the movies.

But Mickey Sharp, 'experienced and successful' teenage detective, wishes it was. Then maybe he wouldn't be trying to solve a case for a demanding female client with only a piece of pink football shirt to go on. And he probably wouldn't be being nagged by a small boy about the return of his missing cat . . .

Mickey Sharp is back with a new mystery. He can wisecrack his way out of most situations at school but it's not going to be that easy to score on this case!

'Stuffed full of hilarious characters, top teen observations and jokes . . . Dominic Barker has played a blinder!'
The Times

ISBN 0 552 546488

CORGI BOOKS

JOHNNY AND THE DEAD
Terry Pratchett

Sell the cemetery? Over their dead bodies . . .

Not many people can see the dead (not many would want to). Twelve-year-old Johnny Maxwell can. And he's got bad news for them: the council want to sell the cemetery as a building site. But the dead have learnt a thing or two from Johnny. They're not going to take it lying down . . . especially since it's Halloween tomorrow.

Besides, they're beginning to find that life is a lot more fun than it was when they were . . . well . . . alive. Particularly if they break a few rules . . .

'Terry Pratchett uses his wicked sense of humour to hilarious effect in this new fantasy story . . . anyone over ten can find something to smile about here'
Daily Mail

ISBN 0 552 52740 8

Now available from all good book stores

CORGI BOOKS

SOLO ACT
Helen Dunwoodie

*Iris has the looks, the voice, the confidence . . .
So why is everything going wrong for her?*

First Jimmy Garcia, the new (and *very*
fanciable) director of her drama group has
the nerve to criticise her acting. In front of
everyone! Then, when he announces his plan
to take their show to the world-famous
Edinburgh Fringe Festival, Iris's mother
starts being really difficult about her going.

Iris *knows* she's good enough to make it –
and knows that stardom doesn't come easy.
But why does it have to be *so* hard?

**'Dunwoodie sweeps the reader along in a
most agreeable and enjoyable way'**
Books for Keeps

**'An all-round excellent read for the stage-
struck and those looking for a deeper
acount of human relationships'**
Carousel

ISBN 0 552 54524 4

Now available from all good book stores

CORGI BOOKS